My name is Callum Ormond.
I am fifteen
and I am a hunted fugitive...

CONSPIRACY 365

365

BOOK TWO: FEBRUARY

To Hélène, Jessica and Sam

First American Paperback Edition 2012
First American Edition 2010
Kane Miller, A Division of EDC Publishing

Text copyright © Gabrielle Lord, 2010
Cover design copyright © Scholastic Australia, 2010
Illustrations copyright © Scholastic Australia, 2010
Back cover photo of boy's face © Scholastic Australia, 2010
Cover photo of boy © Scholastic Australia, 2010
Cover design by Natalie Winter
Illustrations by Rebecca Young

First published by Scholastic Australia Pty Limited in 2010
This edition published under licence from Scholastic Australia Pty Limited

Library of Congress Control Number: 2009934733

Printed and bound in the United States of America
4 5 6 7 8 9 10
ISBN: 978-1-61067-104-0

CONSPIRACY 365

BOOK TWO: FEBRUARY

GABRIELLE LORD

Kane Miller
A DIVISION OF EDC PUBLISHING

PREVIOUSLY . . .

31 DECEMBER
I'm chased by a madman, who tells me my dad was murdered and that I will be too if I don't hide out until midnight, next December 31st. *365 days . . .*

1 JANUARY
I somehow survive a boating accident during a violent storm in shark-infested waters.

2 JANUARY
Our house gets broken into and trashed.

9 JANUARY
Some woman calls me claiming to have information on my dad. But before we meet, I'm kidnapped and interrogated by a group of criminals.

10 JANUARY

After narrowly escaping my captors, my uncle and little sister are brutally attacked. Rafe is recovering in the hospital, and Gabbi's on life support. *My* face is on the news as the attacker! The police are after me now too! I've got no choice but to run.

13 JANUARY

I'm hiding out in a dump at St. Johns Street, trying to make sense of the crazy drawings Dad did just before he died, and trying to figure out a way to clear my name.

31 JANUARY

I'm grabbed off the street by another criminal gang, this time led by the infamous Vulkan Sligo. When he realizes I have no information to give him, he traps me in a fast-filling, underground oil tank . . . and leaves me there to drown . . .

1 FEBRUARY

334 days to go . . .

Car Lot

12:00 am

The stinking sump oil gushed out of the cable on my right, relentlessly filling the underground tank I was trapped in. I struggled to hold my mouth above the rising tide as I bashed my slippery fists against the manhole cover over my head. It was useless. It wouldn't budge.

Car wheels screeched and sped away in the distance, reminding me that I was completely alone. Left to die.

12:03 am

No matter how hard I tried to move around in the thick, glue-like oil, I couldn't stop it from climbing my face. My mouth was almost completely covered. I shut it tight. I desperately pushed my head back and forced my nostrils —

my last chance at life — up and away from the surface that was swallowing me whole.

You've got to slow down your breathing, I told myself. I knew it would be certain death if my nose started sucking up the oil. The powerful, caustic fumes burned through my insides like acid. My head spun, and fear made me breathe faster and harder.

My own voice, from moments ago, played back in my mind . . . *Red hair. Purple sunglasses.* But I'd never even seen the woman who'd abducted me, so what in the world had made me say that to Sligo?!

And even more puzzling, he seemed to know who I was talking about — he knew someone from the conference that fit that exact description! What was going on?

I had escaped death at sea just a month ago, only to find myself facing it again. But there was no possible escape from this.

12:04 am

The oil reached the bottom of my nose. Any moment now and it would block my nostrils entirely . . . I strained my muscles harder, trying to lift my body even just a quarter of an inch higher, but it was impossible. There was nowhere to go.

I started inhaling droplets of oil. *365 days* . . . the crazy guy's deranged warning from New Year's Eve screamed through my head, taunting me. I'd only made it through one month — whatever lethal force had cursed my family *had* finally gotten to me. A few more seconds, and I wouldn't be able to breathe . . . I closed my eyes and hoped it would be quick.

12:05 am

I was so intensely focused on letting myself die calmly that I didn't hear the exact moment the gushing stopped. But for some reason, it *had* stopped. Somehow, the flow had been turned off!

Some sort of miracle had put an end to the process. What had happened? I was shaking all over. I was almost completely submerged in oil, but I was alive . . .

I opened my eyes, still straining to keep my nostrils higher than the level of the oil, and listened . . .

Nothing.

I slowly pulled up my arm, trying to avoid making a wave that would swamp my face, and thumped on the cover above me.

I pushed myself closer into the corner, hoping to exert more pressure. But it was a waste of energy. Yeah, the oil may have stopped, but I was just as trapped as I was before.

12:09 am

The relief I'd felt a moment ago started turning into horror. I was stupid to think that the end of the gushing oil meant I'd survived, and that someone had come to my rescue. I was no closer to making it unless I got out.

My mind raced. Maybe it would have been better for the tank to fill completely, so that I could have at least drowned quickly. Now I was going to be stuck in the darkness of the tank and die of asphyxiation or worse, slowly and painfully from thirst!

I strained to listen for a sign of hope outside my oil-filled tomb, but all I could hear in the silence was the beating of my blood against my eardrums — the thumping of my fighting heart.

How was I going to get out of this?

12:18 am

"Hey!"

A *voice*?

"You in the tank," it continued. "You OK?"

OK? Someone was asking me if I was OK? Was I hearing things? I was so light-headed from fumes and adrenaline that I wasn't sure of anything. I wanted to yell out, but there was no way I could open my mouth. I had to make *some* noise, somehow, to let whoever was out there know I was still alive. I was terrified I'd miss my chance — if it even was a chance — and be left there for dead when I was so close to making it.

I took a slow, careful breath through my nose, shut my eyes tight, and thumped at the manhole cover with my fists. Oil splashed all over my face.

I stopped and waited.

I knew I couldn't hold my breath much longer.

Just as I was giving up on the hope of air, there was a creaking, grinding noise. Someone was twisting open the cover!

It lifted, and soft light fell on the sea of black surrounding me. I hauled myself up the ladder and out the opening, spitting and gasping. I'd freed my mouth and nostrils from the deadly tide and re-emerged into life.

I coughed and wheezed uncontrollably, madly shaking my oil-soaked head. I clung to the ground above me while my lower half hung exhausted below me, still in the tank and submerged in oil.

"Who's there?" I finally managed to croak, spitting oil from my lips.

No answer.

"Hello?" I asked again, cautiously looking around.

Was I imagining things? Was this some trick, or some sort of mental torture that Vulkan Sligo was playing with?

"Why don't you pull yourself out already? Or do you like hanging out in there?"

There was no mistake, it was a voice. The voice of a girl. I struggled to climb a little higher. My clothes and shoes were heavy and saturated, and my feet skidded, banging my shins hard into the ladder.

Eventually I crawled all the way out of the tank and rolled over onto my back, exhausted.

Something loomed in my vision. I blinked and tried to focus.

Above me stood the girl I'd seen earlier in the office with Sligo, the one with the strange eye makeup and wild hair. She stared down at me with her shadowed, almond-shaped eyes.

"Who are you?" I asked, groggily. "Did you turn the oil off?"

"Look at you," she said, pointing down at me. "You look like a swamp monster!"

What?

"Actually, your eyes and forehead are still human. Kind of!" she laughed.

After all I'd been through, this girl was cracking jokes? I started lifting myself to my feet, trying to think of something clever to throw back at her, but instead I slipped and fell, landing heavily on my side.

I sat back up to hear more laughter. The girl was laughing at me again!

"You should see yourself!" she said, as I crawled away from the tank. "Believe me, it's funny!"

I tried to stand up again, and this time the girl grabbed my flailing right hand with a surprisingly strong grip, and steadied me. As I balanced myself so I could stand without her help, one of my greasy sneakers skidded out from under me, and I crashed down again.

The girl was still gripping my hand, so she came down too and fell awkwardly on top of me. At least that stopped her laughing.

She scrambled to her feet and scrunched up her face in disgust. Her hands and clothes were covered in oil too.

"Look what you've done!" she yelled.

"Just like a swamp monster," I jeered. "You should see *your*self!"

She looked down, unsuccessfully trying to rub the black muck off.

"I've gotta get this off me," she said, turning and running towards a building behind the office where I'd been interrogated. I followed, squelching after her.

12:38 am

We were in some sort of laundry room. The girl was washing her face over a big steel tub. A cracked mirror hung above the sink I was standing in front of, and I was shocked to see my reflection. The whites of my eyes stared out of a messy, black head, and oil crawled down my face in gluey streams and dripped onto the floor.

My heart rate started to slow down a little. I was alive, and I was out.

"You're not going to get very far looking like that," she warned, peering up at me with dark, smudged eyes. "You'd better be quick if you want to clean up, they'll be back soon to fish your body out of the tank, and if they find you here instead of there, you're not the only one who'll be in trouble."

She rushed around and kept looking past me towards the door. Although she had a pretty face, her eyes were cold and unsmiling. But for some reason, she'd stuck around to save my life.

"OK," I said, "but I have to grab my backpack first."

"I've already helped enough. I'm getting out of here the second I've cleaned up. You're on your own."

I quickly washed some of the oil off my face. I knew I didn't have long to get the answers I needed, but surely this stranger could tell me *something* . . .

"What's your story?" I asked her. "What are you doing with Vulkan Sligo, and why did you help me?"

She wiped her face hurriedly with a towel. "You want to know why I helped you?" she asked. Clearly she didn't want to answer the first part of my question.

"I helped because . . . I liked your piercings," she said.

"You saved my life because of my *studs*?" I quickly felt around to see if my fake studs were even still there. And then I remembered Gabbi's Celtic ring and felt frantically for it on my hand. Relieved, I found it clinging on tight.

"You got a problem with that?" she threatened. "What does it matter, anyway? You're alive, aren't ya? Isn't that enough?"

This girl was unbelievable.

"You'd better hurry up if you want to *stay* alive," she added. "I'm serious, Sligo will be back any minute, and if he sees me — " she paused and slung her bag over her shoulder, "he'll know it was me who got you out. We can't let that happen. He can't even find out that I *knew* you were in the tank."

"I get it," I said. She didn't need to warn me. I knew all about danger. Sligo had just left me to drown. I knew what he was capable of. "But first we need to get back into the office to grab my bag."

The girl brushed down her damp skirt. "*We?* I'm sorry, but like I just said, I don't have time. I don't want to end up in the oil tank like you. I don't think I'd have anyone coming to *my* rescue."

She grabbed her scarf from the sink and headed for the door.

"Wait! Who are you? Why did you help me?"

She pushed past me on her way out, slowing briefly in the doorway. "Look, I can wait a few minutes for you down the road. But it's too dangerous for me to hang around here any longer. If you do get away before Sligo comes back, don't go through the main entrance, use the small gate in the back corner of the lot." She looked at her watch, then started running, turning briefly to yell back, "I'm only waiting a few minutes, got it?"

"But my bag," I shouted, "the office is locked!"

Her voice drifted back. "There's a spare key on top of the window frame!"

12:52 am

I ran around to the stairs in front of the office, leaving dark, wet footprints behind me. I hurried to the porch and stretched up, feeling along the top of the window frame to my right.

Nothing.

There was the sound of an approaching car. It had to be Sligo or his thugs, coming back to collect my body.

I launched up towards the top of the left window frame, and my scrabbling fingers finally lucked onto a key. I almost dropped it — I was still slipping everywhere — but somehow I managed to unlock the door. My backpack was exactly where I'd seen it last — shoved in the trash can. I lunged and snatched it, and in one move I was outside again.

The sound of the approaching car had stopped. The lot looked deserted. Maybe it hadn't been Sligo coming back after all.

I kicked off my oil-drenched jeans and pulled on another pair from my bag, struggling to drag them over my wet skin. I threw on my hoodie and began running, hoping this wasn't the kind of place that had bloodthirsty dogs prowling around.

A powerful, automatic light suddenly flooded the area. I swung around and realized that I was standing, startled stiff, in headlights! The car *was* right there behind me!

I started running again. The brilliant headlights shifted and followed me as the car drove further into the lot.

Two men jumped out and came after me on foot. I bolted away, counting on finding the gate that the girl had told me to use. I kept low as I scrambled over rusty car parts, engines and other bits of machinery, until finally I spotted the gate in the wire fence.

I broke cover and made a run for it.

1:01 am

The thugs shouted and thundered behind me. I put my head down and drove my legs as hard as I could.

When I'd made it a few hundred yards from the gate, I slowed down a little, scanning the street for the girl. She suddenly emerged from the bushes.

"Run!" I yelled. "They're coming!"

Without a word she joined me, and we both pounded along the road together, turning up and down streets without even thinking — anything to get as far away as possible from that place. Away from Sligo. Away from the oil tank. Away from danger.

1:23 am

Eventually the sound of our pursuers dropped off, and we stopped running. I leaned heavily against a brick wall, trying to catch my breath. The girl had also stopped and was panting nearby. She looked down at the palms of her hands, and I noticed under the thin stream of street light that they were red, swollen and blistered. She must have hurt them turning off the oil.

She suddenly looked up and caught me staring at her hands.

"And you haven't even said thanks," she snapped.

1:25 am

"Believe me," I pleaded. "I'm grateful. Thanks . . . I don't even know your name."

She ignored me and started walking off. She *had* saved my life, so if she wanted silence I'd let her have it. For now.

We loped along together, and I hoped we'd put enough distance between us and the Slug for the time being. I was sweating from the heat of the night and all of that hard running. What a life.

"I know *your* name," she suddenly said, raising her eyes and shifting her embroidered shoulder bag from one side to the other. "Everyone in the city knows your name. Sligo certainly does."

Closer up I could see green-gold flecks in her dark eyes. I also noticed that her wild and wavy hair had little sparkles in it.

"I know," I said. But what did she mean by that? Sligo didn't seem like the sort of guy who'd be interested in a teenage fugitive, and there was only one reason why he'd be interested in me — somehow, he must have known something about my dad's life-changing discovery. Sligo already knew about the Angel, a jewel and the Riddle. Maybe something had been leaked to him from the conference in Ireland.

1:32 am

We'd stopped again, and everything was still and quiet, except for the crickets. I felt like I was shaking all over. It must have been some sort of delayed shock.

We were surrounded by suburban houses. I was sure all the families inside would have long ago been tucked into bed. I thought of Mum, sleepless in our house suburbs away, and Gabbi on life support, alone in the hospital. Mum had almost lost our whole family — first Dad, Gabbi in a way, and now me. I wanted my old life back so badly and wished I wasn't this hunted kid, on the run, living in a derelict dump, trying to stay one jump ahead of . . . of everyone.

"I overhear things," said the girl, suddenly interrupting my thoughts. "I know you've got something Sligo wants."

I looked down the long street. "You know what that is?" I asked. It would be great if this girl had a few real answers for me.

She shook her head, and the glitter in her hair flashed. "Only that it's massive, and that he'll stop at nothing to get it."

"So I've noticed."

"But I knew you didn't know anything about it," she said, matter-of-factly. "You would have told him if you did. Anybody would have . . . over drowning in sump oil."

Finally something straightforward that I could agree with. "You seem to know so much about me. It's hardly fair, I don't even know your name," I said, hoping for the straight talk to continue. I was careful — I didn't want to scare her off. I owed her for shutting off the oil pump, and there were so many questions I needed to ask. Not just about Sligo and what he knew about my dad, but about her. She'd helped me — saved my life — but what was she doing with Sligo? I couldn't figure her out. She was nothing like the girls I knew from school. But, as strange as she was, she was company, and it felt good to have someone around to talk to . . . someone who wasn't trying to kill me.

"I'll tell you my name when we get there," she said.

"Get where? I thought we were just getting *away*."

"Now you're going to help *me*."

"Is that right? You could have just asked for my help," I suggested. "Nobody likes being bossed around, especially not by some nameless girl."

With one hand on her hip, she stared back at me with intense eyes. "All right. My name is Winter," she said. "Winter Frey. Happy?"

"Fancy name," I said.

"Fancy suits me," she replied.

I was trying to think of something funny to say back when a car turned onto the road ahead, about a block away. I didn't wait to see if it was the black Subaru, I just grabbed Winter's hand and hauled her off the sidewalk and into a bushy driveway. I let go of her, but not before noticing a tiny tattoo of a bird on the inside of her left wrist. She pulled away quickly, protectively folding her arms, and we both huddled down, sneaking glimpses of the car slowly rolling past.

"Sligo's car," she hissed.

We waited, hidden in the darkness, until we were sure that the car had gone. Winter looked around. "Let's go."

1:49 am

My body felt wrecked. My face was swollen from being roughed up, my shins and arms were aching from the struggle in the tank, and my old injury in my right shoulder pinched, making sure I hadn't forgotten it. I kept seeing Winter's bird tattoo in my mind, wondering what she was doing roaming the streets with me — some fugitive kid — in the middle of the night.

"What are you doing with Vulkan Sligo?" I finally asked again. I'd wasted enough time trying to imagine a reason why a girl like that would have anything to do with a guy like him.

Winter turned to me under the shelter of a large tree. I kept my eyes on the street, scanning for any sign of movement.

"You really wanna know?"

"That's what I said."

"The answer is simple. He's my guardian."

"Your guardian? What do you mean? Where are your parents?"

Around us, the air was suddenly very still and cold.

"You ask too many questions," she said.

"I'm only after basic information."

"Get it somewhere else. OK?"

I shrugged.

"And," she resumed, "even though he's my guardian, there's no way I'd hang around him unless —"

"Unless what?" I interrupted. "Is it because you're some kind of outlaw too? Birds of a feather flock together?" I looked again for the tiny bird on her wrist.

She shook her hair, and a million tiny sparkles flashed. "I have my reasons. Very good reasons that I don't have to explain to anyone. And he needs me. Even if only to help him change his image."

"Change his image? He wants to go straight? Is that what you're trying to tell me?" I couldn't believe what I was hearing. "He almost *murdered* me a moment ago, and now you're telling me he wants to change his image? Too funny!"

"It might sound like a joke to you, but there's one thing you should know about Sligo. He has ambitions. He doesn't like being called a criminal by the media."

"He *is* a criminal! Forget what the media does or doesn't call him!"

"You've got to understand, he doesn't see it like that. He's desperate to be seen as straight — respectable. That was the whole reason he was interested in you."

"So interested he wants to drown me? I'm not getting you, Winter."

"He wanted to use you somehow, and well, obviously his plans didn't exactly work out. Look, I don't have to justify anything to you. Just believe me when I tell you that this massive thing he's chasing — the reason for the interrogation — it's all tied up with his pathetic attempt to eventually be . . . respected and admired. That's all there really is to it."

The Ormond Singularity, I thought. Did it have the power to make the crooked straight?

"Sometimes I suspect he's only using *me*," Winter continued. "My family is — was — very wealthy. We owned property from the highlands right down to Dolphin Point. My parents were both very successful and well known . . . in their circles."

She hesitated, and I sensed something like a deep sorrow that had been frozen over. "Sligo used to work for my father," her voice faltered, "before the accident."

Her voice trailed off.

"The accident?" I asked, cautiously.

"I don't want to talk about it," she said, cutting me off. Her eyes cooled again in an instant, and she flashed them in warning at me.

An accident that took both of her parents? I wanted to ask, but I stopped myself — she'd made it clear that the subject was too painful. She suddenly didn't seem quite so fearless. It was bad enough losing Dad — but I still had Mum. Kind of.

"Answer me something," she said, interrupting my thoughts.

"Do you always talk like that?" I asked. "Like you're commanding an army?"

Winter flung her head to one side. "It's just a simple question. Are you any good at breaking into houses?"

Mansfield Way, Dolphin Point

2:02 am

We'd arrived in front of a huge house which was set back quite a distance from the road. The property was encased in bushes and a tall, intimidating, black iron fence. It was number 113, according to the polished brass numbers on the gate. The neighboring houses were just as huge and daunting, but they were all lined up in perfect unison — polished and proud — unlike this place that seemed a little overgrown and unkempt.

I turned to Winter. "You want to break into this?" I asked, exhausted. "No way. You must be out of your mind. It's probably covered in cameras."

She looked me up and down. "It's not as secure as it looks," she said, slipping open the gate with ease. "See? And anyway, maybe I should have phrased that better," she said. "I'm really just visiting a friend."

"Right," I said, "and does your 'friend' know you're coming?"

"Well, actually . . . so it's not exactly a visit."

"So, what is it?"

"It's a — I guess you can really only call it a break-in," she said. "There's something in there that I have to get, and I'd really *appreciate* it if you joined me."

That's just great, I thought. Here I was already on the run, having survived a murder attempt, with criminals after me, cops after me, and now this girl wanted me to help her break into a Dolphin Point mansion?

"What's your problem?" she asked icily, as her eyes narrowed. "I saved your life, remember? And according to the media, you've already attempted murder. Twice. Psycho-teen, they're calling you. What's a little break-in compared with that? If you don't want to help me, I can just call *my* Sligo, and have his thugs here in five minutes. You can't run very far in five minutes."

What was with this girl, threatening me?! Had she only saved me so that she could use me? Was she nothing but a user like Sligo?

"Anyway," she said, quickly sensing my changing mood, "it's not a robbery." She pulled me through the gate after her. "The girl who's living here has something important that belonged to my mum. I just need to get what's mine."

"And why doesn't your mum ask for it back?" I asked, knowing it was sure to upset her. But as soon as the words came out of my mouth, I wished I could take them back.

Winter looked away, but not before I'd recognized the sharp blow of grief that hit her face. She grabbed my hoodie and wrenched me down behind a line of thick bushes. "My mum can't ask for anything," she whispered firmly in my ear. "My mum's dead."

I pulled away from her grip.

"I'm sorry," I whispered.

Winter shrugged.

"I shouldn't have said that . . . I know how you feel," I offered.

Winter glared at me. "You *know*? What would *you* know about it! You're just some stiff suburban school kid who's suddenly stumbled into some trouble. You think you're an expert now?! Ha!"

"Look," I said, "keep it down. Do you want us to get caught out here already?" I felt no need whatsoever to explain myself to her.

I could see her trying to figure out what to say. Her eyes narrowed as she spoke, "Anyway," she said, "the guy that lives here — the boyfriend — works as a bodyguard for Murray Durham —"

"Murray Durham?!" I cut her off, hoping there was some mistake. "He's a bigger crim' than Sligo! You know how he got his nickname 'Toe Cutter,' don't you? It's pretty self-explanatory."

This was getting worse by the minute. Winter Frey was connecting me with another bad guy. I never thought I'd actually be talking to someone who knew both Vulkan Sligo and Toe Cutter Durham . . . although, ever since the run-in with that crazy guy back home on New Year's Eve, all I seemed to know was bad guys.

"Durham and Sligo were friends a really long time ago, but now they're mortal enemies. I can't be caught having anything to do with anyone even remotely connected to Durham. Sligo would disown me. My life depends on it . . . well, my allowance depends on it." Winter leaned forward and peered around the bushes towards the house. "I probably need Sligo now just as much as he needs me."

"Pocket money?" I asked.

She stifled a laugh. "You could call it that. Anyway," she added, "it's easier doing it this way. To cut a long story short, my locket ended up with the bodyguard's girlfriend. I've been inside plenty of times before, and I know exactly where it is."

The word "locket" sent the hairs on the back of my neck prickling. Sligo had asked me about a piece of jewelry — and someone had stolen jewelry from Dad's suitcase. Was this just a coincidence? Had this girl somehow gotten hold of it?

"And the locket's yours?" I asked her.

"That's what I just said. My mum and dad left it for me, for my tenth birthday."

"So you didn't get it recently?"

"No!" she said, rolling her eyes. "Do I look like I turned ten yesterday? What is this, an interrogation, or are you just a really bad listener? Anyway, the problem we have right now is the bodyguard. He's probably out working . . . but I'm not sure of that."

"So we're breaking into Toe Cutter's bodyguard's house, and he could be in there waiting for us?"

Winter nodded. "Who's a clever boy?" she said, in her mocking way. "That's *exactly* it. Enough chitchat, let's get this thing over with."

2:08 am

We were slowly approaching the huge double front doors, creeping up behind the bushes that lined the long driveway, when Winter tugged my arm, pulling me back. "Not that way," she hissed. "Follow me."

She led me around the side of the house, past huge curtained windows, until we came to a short flight of steps leading to a smaller door. She pulled out a credit card, slipped it between the door and the lock, gave it a deft tweak, and silently pressed it open.

I was impressed. Maybe I could learn a thing or two from her.

We crept into the house and stole down the hall. I could hear the sound of a TV, and I tapped Winter's shoulder. She turned to me, finger on her lips, and gestured ahead.

In the family room that opened up at the end of the hallway, a man — the bodyguard, I guessed — his back to us, was sprawled on a black leather recliner in front of a huge plasma screen. On the thick white rug at his feet, slept the girl, curled up like a cat.

Winter pointed to the door on the other side of the room. We were going to have to sneak behind them and cross the room to get over there.

The guy was watching some war movie with lots of loud explosions, gunfire and shouting. I wondered how the girl was sleeping through it. He seemed engrossed in the action, but I didn't want to think about what he might do if he turned around and found two young intruders in his house.

Using the volume of the TV as cover, Winter and I pressed close against the wall and snuck through the family room, step by stealthy step. We slid our way along, silently passing only a foot or so behind the guy watching the movie. We had almost made it to the other side of the room when he suddenly turned — luckily, not our way. Instead, he glanced down the empty hallway we'd just crept through. Had he heard something?

Terrified that he would look around and see us, we froze, but a child's scream from the movie ripped his attention back to the screen.

After passing the last part of the wall, we slipped through the door and up some stairs. I trailed Winter along a dimly lit, carpeted corridor, passing several closed doors and some huge vases with spiky plants growing out of them. Winter seemed to know exactly where to go.

After ducking into one of the rooms, Winter quickly closed the door behind us and then switched on a lamp. The light revealed a very girly bedroom. The walls and curtains were a soft pink, and the lace-white bed was covered in pillows in every shade of pink you could imagine. Gabbi would have loved it.

Winter went straight for the dressing table, which was topped with a delicate, glass-framed mirror. She opened the top drawer and pulled out a red velvet music box. Within seconds, she'd silently lifted out a small, silver, heart-shaped locket on a long chain. With a look of triumph, she pocketed it, nodded to me, switched off the lamp, and carefully opened the door again.

We hurried out of the room and back down the staircase, treading softly on the carpet. We didn't need to go back through the family room, so I hoped getting out of the house was going to be easier than getting in.

2:20 am

Winter opened the front door, but it slipped from her grasp and a gust of wind banged it against the wall behind it.

"Who's there?!"

"What is it, hon?" came the girl's voice, dazed and sleepy on the rug.

"Someone's in the house!"

I didn't hesitate. This time *I* grabbed Winter and dragged her out the front door, down the path and out number 113's gate as fast as I could, only letting go of her wrist when we'd reached the street.

Her footsteps flew beside me as we raced along the road, taking left turns, then right, then left, until finally, when it was safe, we both fell exhausted onto the grass of a tiny, moonlit park.

We both puffed and panted, looking up at the sky.

"That door!" she said, sitting up. "I forgot it slams!"

She buried her hands into her skirt pockets and pulled out two chocolate bars. She waved one around in front of me. I sat up and snatched it from her, tearing off the wrapper.

"Thanks, where'd you get these?"

"Let's just say I know where my *friend* keeps her chocolate stash, too," she replied with a grin.

"It was pretty clear you'd been in there before."

"I grew up in that house," she said.

I remembered how she'd described her rich family before. "Really?" I said. "I've got an uncle who lives in this suburb too."

2:41 am

Winter's cell phone rang, and she jumped up and took it out of her bag. I watched her move away and wondered who was calling her at this hour.

"I'm getting a drink," I said, as Winter returned. I stood up on my aching legs and stumbled over to a water fountain in the middle of the park. I had a long drink and splashed water over my face and neck, trying to cool down. As I straightened up, I found myself wondering how I could find out whether her story about the locket was true. Her sad eyes seemed so real, but there was something untrustworthy about her. I took another drink before heading back to where she sat on the grass, determined to find out more. In the glow of the tall park light, I found Winter sitting there, sifting through my backpack!

"Hey! Stop it!" I shouted, hurrying towards her. "What are you doing? You can't do that! Get your hands off my stuff!"

Everything was scattered all over the grass, including Dad's drawings and the tracing paper I found in his suitcase with the words "G'managh" and "Kilfane." I was furiously snatching my stuff from the ground when I noticed that she was sitting there quietly grinning. She held one of the angel drawings in her hands.

"Give me that!" I tried to grab it out of her hand, but she jerked it out of my reach.

I was about to give her a piece of my mind

when I noticed her eyes. For the first time, they seemed alive and shining. She pointed to the Angel and pointed to my dad's letter.

"Where did this come from?" she asked. "Do you know him too?"

"The Angel?" I asked. "You know about the Angel?" A sudden surge of excitement smothered my anger.

"Of course I do! I know where he is. I've seen him lots of times!"

What was she talking about? Everybody in the whole stinking world seemed to be asking questions about the Angel, and this girl was claiming she knew all about him!

"How long have you known about him?" she asked.

"I don't know about him, I've just got this picture that my dad drew. Why? What do you know? What does it mean?"

I didn't like the way Winter was handling Dad's drawing as if she owned it, so I snatched it away from her.

Winter's face resumed its usual cool, superior, stuff-you expression.

"Please," I urged. "Tell me everything you know about it."

"Why? What's it to you?"

I sat back down on the grass again. "My dad drew that angel not long before he died."

The atmosphere immediately changed between us.

"Your dad's dead?" she asked.

I nodded.

Winter carefully pulled the locket out of her pocket. "Now you understand," she said, in a softer voice, "why this is so important to me."

I did. I understood the way she clutched the locket, like it was the final word from a lost friend. It was the way *I* held Dad's drawings.

"You lost your dad, too, didn't you?" I asked.

Tears began to fill her eyes. She looked away without speaking . . . but I had my answer.

I wasn't lying when I said I knew how she felt. What kind of accident took the lives of both her mother *and* her father? I also knew that now wasn't the time to try and find out.

She remained silently turned away from me for a few moments, then she took the locket, opened it, and passed it to me. Inside were two tiny photos. One was of an Asian man with black hair — whose intense eyes tilted up in the same way as Winter's — and next to that, there was a photo of a fair-haired woman who had the same delicate chin as Winter.

Little Bird

"You look a lot like both of your parents," I said, turning the locket over.

"Really?" she asked. "It's hard to look like one or the other when your mum's so fair and your dad's Chinese."

On the back of the silver heart were the delicately engraved words "Little Bird" beneath a Chinese character.

At that moment, her phone rang again. She took the locket back, then walked away to take the call.

I waited, wondering about her excitement at seeing the angel drawing, wondering what had happened to her parents. Did she have a connection to the Ormond Angel? Winter owed me a lot of answers, but I knew I'd have to be very careful and patient.

I couldn't hear what she was saying, but it wasn't long before she was off the phone and back to me.

She looked me straight in the eyes. "I've gotta go," she said. "He's hassling me again."

"Sligo?"

"Thank goodness for cell phones," she said. "He thinks I'm at home. Clearly he's in a rage because you've disappeared, but he doesn't suspect I've had anything to do with it. Thank goodness. He likes to think he can keep tabs on me. As if. If only he knew where I really was, and who I was really with!"

"Listen," I said quickly, not wanting the opportunity to slip by. "I've got to find out about this angel. It's really important." Even though I wasn't sure about this girl, I could feel the excitement growing in me at the thought of such an awesome break — I could have been on the verge of finding out one of the secrets hidden in Dad's drawings.

"First, you've gotta tell me why it's so important to you," she said. "You tell me that, and I'll show you the angel *I* know."

This girl hung out with criminals and broke into other people's houses. Was she telling the truth?

Winter was already walking away before I realized she was leaving.

"Hey! Come back!" I yelled after her.

"Only if you tell me why that angel is so important," she called out. "Why Sligo is willing to kill to get information about it."

I didn't know what to say. If I told her about the Ormond Singularity and its connection to my dad's drawings, she could go straight to Sligo and tell him everything. I really wanted to trust her, but what I knew about her was telling me not to.

I jumped up and raced after her, catching her just before she'd reached the street a short distance away.

"You've gotta tell me where I can find that angel!"

She turned around and tossed her hair away from her face. "I don't *gotta* do anything. No one tells *me* what to do. You call me," she said, "when you're ready to deal. Then I'll consider it."

She turned and hurried away.

"I don't even have your number!"

"Check your phone, Callum Ormond!"

I ran to my backpack and pulled out my phone. It slid open to a new screensaver. Winter by moonlight, complete with a new phone number in my contacts list.

Hideout
38 St. Johns Street

6:05 am

The birds were just beginning to call from the trees in the street as I crawled under the house and climbed up through the hole in the floorboards. The place smelled pretty foul and stuffy, so I opened the back door to get some fresh air inside.

I hadn't realized how starving I was until I started eating. I ended up plowing through half a loaf of stale bread.

I couldn't stop thinking about whether I could trust Winter. I desperately needed to find the angel that she said she knew about, but I couldn't bring myself to confide in her. I already had enough problems with Sligo and the woman who'd first abducted and interrogated me, who, for some reason, was stuck in my mind as a redhead. I couldn't risk them finding out anything more.

The little Celtic ring Gabbi had given me glinted on my finger. "Get well, little Gabster," I whispered, imagining her lying asleep in her intensive care bed.

I pulled out my sleeping bag and crashed.

2:01 pm

"Dude, you're alive," Boges said, after I answered my phone.

"Only just."

"I was trying to call you last night, but you must have been out of range. What happened, where were you?"

"Oh, long story . . ." I sighed, sitting up and stretching. The car lot was already a long ago, hazy blur.

"Nothing would shock me anymore. You could tell me anything and I'd believe it."

I could hear Mrs. Michalko calling him in the background.

"Look, I've gotta get off, Mum's coming," he said. "I'll drop by as soon as I can, OK?"

2 FEBRUARY

333 days to go . . .

5:17 pm

I'd spent the day holed up in the St. Johns dump, trying again to make sense of the drawings and hoping Boges would show up. I heard a couple of people talking and laughing as they walked by outside on the street, while I lurked in the dark, shifting around like a cockroach.

My plans for visiting my great-uncle in Mount Helicon had completely fallen apart, thanks to Sligo, and while I really wanted to get out there and hopefully find some answers, I thought I was probably better off staying put for a few days.

Winter's phone always seemed to be turned off, which was driving me nuts. What was the point of giving me her number if she was never going to take a call from me? I was sick and tired of having so many unanswered questions.

Feeling isolated and alone, I wished I could go home. I called Mum once and left a message on her voicemail just so I could hear her voice and she could hear mine. I told her I was safe and not to worry.

I thought again of my little sister, stuck in a hospital bed while security watched out for her fifteen-year-old brother . . . They needed to be protecting her from people like the psycho woman and Sligo, who were all determined to discover Dad's secret and who were willing to take out anyone in their path.

It wasn't fair. I'd done nothing wrong, but I was serving a sentence of solitary confinement, away from the people I needed to watch over. I just needed to stay alive long enough to solve Dad's mystery.

3 FEBRUARY

332 days to go . . .

2:11 am

I kept waking up thinking I could hear Dad's voice calling me.

I tossed and turned, not quite awake, but not quite asleep either. Caught in that half-asleep state, I could see the threadbare toy dog from my nightmares. It hovered in my mind, heavy and bleak. I'd had so many close calls lately that I couldn't understand why or how this image could make me feel so uneasy. Storms at sea, sharks, being thrown in a trunk, almost drowning in oil — they were all terrifying things I *could* understand.

9:33 am

My eyes flew open. Something had completely wrenched me from sleep. I strained my ears to hear a dull thudding that seemed to be coming from outside. Right away I thought of Winter, handing me and my secrets over to Sligo.

I crouched behind one of the boarded-up windows. Someone was definitely creeping around outside. I could hear their careful footsteps crushing the long grass.

I spotted the hole in the floor and dove into it, quickly pulling the carpet back over my head. Buried in dirt and cobwebs, I strained to hear where the footsteps had gone.

They'd stopped. Hunched under the floorboards, I began crawling on all fours straight ahead towards the light and up behind the vegetation that grew around the front porch.

I had to keep my head down low to avoid colliding with the sagging floor above. I cringed as my already aching right shoulder slammed into a pylon.

The light ahead suddenly shifted — disappearing behind a figure crawling towards me! Someone was under the house with me!

Awkwardly, I started backing up. If I could make it back through the hole in the floorboards and drag something heavy over the opening, I'd be able to make a run for it. Unless there was someone waiting up there for me, too.

"Dude? It's me!"

Boges!

"Cal?" he asked.

I peered ahead through the gloom under the house. As the dust settled, I got a shock to find Boges's round face peering right back at me, inches from my face!

"Boges! Who else would be hiding down here in the dark?!"

9:37 am

"You almost gave me a heart attack!" I continued.

"Sorry, dude. There was a police van cruising the street, and I thought this way would be safer. Nice place you've got here," he joked, wiping a sticky cobweb from his face.

Boges laughed at himself as we both pulled ourselves up into the house.

"Something smells good for a change!" I said, as he opened his bag and threw me a squashed paper bag of sandwiches and fries. "And they're still hot!"

"Yes, but don't forget to eat your fruit, young man," he said in his best Mrs. Michalko voice, tossing me a couple of apples and a banana.

"Oh, thanks, Mama M!" I joked.

He pulled his laptop out last, and then we made ourselves comfortable on the floor and started eating.

"What's the latest on Gabbi?" I asked.

Boges stopped chewing. "No change. She's still unconscious. 'Serious but stable.'"

Stable. That word made everything sound a little bit better.

"And Mum?"

Boges made an indecisive groaning sort of sound. "She's *kinda* OK. I went to see her last night. She was complaining about one of your dad's colleagues — Eric somebody — saying how disappointed she was that he hadn't been in touch with her."

"That'd be Eric Blair. He went to Ireland with Dad, but was working on another project."

"He might be helpful to us," suggested Boges. "What's he like?"

"I spoke to him a couple of times on the phone before passing him on to Dad, but that's all. He sounds like a nice guy. Dad seemed to like him. But you're absolutely right, he might be able to tell us more about what happened over there."

"Definitely. So this Eric guy's in your mum's bad books, and as for you, well . . . she's still convinced you've had some sort of breakdown — that you're reacting to all the bad things that have happened to you. She even muttered something about knowing this day would come, and then when I asked her to explain what she meant, she acted like she hadn't said anything. It's weird, dude. I don't know, she just seems so . . . so vacant. It's like she's fighting something in herself, something that's telling her you're innocent. I told her you would never have done anything like that. I told her you *were* innocent, 'Come on, Mrs. O, it's Cal,' and she just sort of patted my arm like she felt sorry for *me*."

Boges looked at me with a helpless face. He started scratching his head. It was like he knew I needed to know what was going on, but he didn't want to be the one to tell me.

"Cal, I tried to tell her that your fingerprints were only on the gun because you picked it up when we were at your uncle's place, but it was useless. I could see she didn't want to listen to me. It's like she figures I'm making up stories to protect you, like I'm being stupid believing that my best friend is being wrongly accused. See, Rafe has said a few things about your 'unstable mental state' and 'recent aggressive behavior' . . . and he's convinced you attacked Gabbi and that you were the one that shot him. How can you argue with that?"

"What's wrong with him? Unstable? Aggressive?

He'd better not be talking about that day in the kitchen! I was just trying to grab *my* mail from him when the stupid idiot fell over himself. I didn't lay a finger on him. He lied about pinching the drawings then, and he's lying about this too."

"But why would he lie about it." said Boges, more like a statement than a question.

"I don't know. I think he's a loser and a liar, but I'd never hurt the guy."

Boges picked up a handful of fries. "Well somebody did."

"And whoever did that to Rafe also put my sister in a coma." I kicked at the leg of a broken chair. "As if I would hurt them!"

"I know, I know, my friend. Chill out. But for whatever reason, that's what he thinks."

"It just doesn't make sense." I put my half-eaten sandwich down. "He's lying. And no one will believe me. Except you. Adults listen to adults. A kid's say means nothing."

"Dude, it's not just a matter of his word. There's the matter of your fingerprints on the weapon."

"Yeah, and like you already said, we both know how they got there. I just don't get it. We know it had to be his gun if it had my fingerprints on it. Maybe he knew something bad was coming. He could have been carrying it with him for protection — oh, what's the point?" I said, frustrated with all the guessing.

We both sat back, staring at the ceiling.

"So . . . I'm afraid to ask . . ." said Boges hesitantly. "What happened to you the other night — you said it was a 'long story?'"

I'd kind of been hoping he wouldn't ask me that question. I sighed and gave him the run-down, starting with the casino explosion after we'd run away from security at the Liberty Mall parking garage, to being tossed like useless trash into the underground oil tank.

11:02 am

"Trapped you in an oil tank!" shouted Boges. "He was trying to drown you?!"

"Hey, keep it down! Yes, an oil tank. I thought I was dead. The oil had fully covered my mouth, and just when I was thinking this is it, someone turned off the pump and the tank stopped filling."

"Who? Who stopped it?"

"A girl."

"A girl?! What?"

"Her name's Winter Frey. She says Vulkan Sligo's her guardian . . ." I could see Boges growing suspicious, fast. "Apparently he used to work for her dad, I don't know how long ago. Her parents were pretty cashed-up, but they both died in some sort of accident, and she's been in the care of the Slug ever since."

"So if she's with him, why did she save you?" Boges wanted to know.

"I don't know." I wanted to know the answer to that question too. "Maybe she just couldn't sit back knowing I was about to die." She must have been watching it happen from a hiding place.

"I think she relies on him to get by," I continued, "but I don't think she's into his big crim' lifestyle — you know, drowning teenagers and stuff. She reckons he's on a serious mission to become acceptable — some sort of pillar of society."

Boges looked like he was about to choke after my "pillar of society" comment.

"I know," I continued, "what kind of pillar of society kills people? But Winter says Sligo believes the Ormond Singularity will make him famous. If he can figure it out. I turned out to be a less-than-helpful source of information for him, but at least I know now that I've got two criminal gangs chasing this thing. Winter says she's willing to help me, but I think she may be doing it to collect favors. Get people in debt to her so that she can call on them when she needs something."

Boges sat back quietly and listened as I explained the break-in to get Winter's locket and the claims she made in the park about recognizing my dad's angel drawings.

"Do you believe her? That she knows where the Angel is?" he asked.

I remembered her shining face. That sort of thing can't be faked.

"I'm convinced of it. She really came alive when she saw the drawings," I said. "She promised she'd take me to see it."

Boges had made himself comfortable on the floor near the wall, his round face serious again. "But she's got an agenda of her own, wanting to know why the Angel is important to you."

"She saved my life, Boges. So I'm willing to take some risk for her — even though she's one weird girl. She's nothing like any of the girls we know, but I kind of like that about her. And anyway, as we've said before, the Angel is important. Dad drew him twice, so I think she's our best chance at the moment."

"She hot?"

"What?"

"Winter. She's hot, isn't she?"

"She's OK," I said, awkwardly. Normally I'd be pretty open with Boges about girls, but something made me want to keep that part of Winter to myself.

Boges gave me a look. "Right. If she starts working things out we could be in real trouble. Be on your guard, dude. We don't want another rival, or enemy, after the same thing. Especially not someone connected to that lunatic Sligo. You've already got two very dangerous enemies."

At least, I thought to myself.

"Try her number again," said Boges.

The mobile phone you have called is turned off. Please try again later.

Boges opened his laptop. "No one knows about this either. Someone chucked it out because it had stopped working, but it only needed a new power box," he said. "The motherboard was fine. But, before we start busting our brains on those drawings again, let's get your profile underway."

"I already have a profile," I said gloomily. "At every cop shop."

"I think you should start a blog," he said. "An appeal to the public could be helpful."

"A blog? Like MySpace?"

"Yeah. A place where you can try and get across your side of the story and shut down all the crazy stuff the media's saying about you. Nobody has to see you or know where you are. They can just read what you have to say and judge for themselves."

"Great idea. Boges, you're a genius."

"I know."

"And modest, too."

For a second it was like the old days, when I was just another kid messing around with a friend. But that feeling didn't last long. At least I had a little hope, and a chance to tell the world of my innocence.

1:04 pm

In the time it took to set up my profile, I'd forgotten about tricky Winter, until I looked over at my phone and saw her face looking up at me. I stretched my leg out and carefully kicked it under my bag.

"I can't stay much longer," Boges reminded me, glancing at his watch. "I've already skipped all my morning classes. Don't want to start bringing in too many notes *from Mum* this term."

Boges could forge his mother's signature perfectly.

I never thought I would envy someone going to

school, but I would have done anything to be packing my bag and heading off with Boges. I'd happily have sat through the "Welcome Back" assembly in the auditorium — all the "over-the-holiday updates" and "hopes for the year ahead" speeches — that normally would have bored me to tears. I'd even have happily sat through one of Mr. Lloyd's biology classes, listening to him drawl on and on about lab safety in his boring, monotone voice while I helped Boges conduct his own little groundbreaking experiments in the back. Or Mrs. Hartley's English class, and her long-winded soliloquies on Shakespeare and poetry.

"I don't think anyone wants to hear my side of the story," I said. "The cops have made up their minds about me already, and we both know that Mum and Rafe think I'm some sort of dangerous nut case."

"They're worried about you, that's for sure," said Boges.

"And I'm worried about Mum. I can't help but wish Rafe would keep away from her."

"I guess she relies on him now that your dad's gone," said Boges. "And he *is* your dad's brother."

"Just because he looks exactly the same as Dad," I said, "doesn't mean anything. Whenever he's around, bad things happen. He pinched the drawings and lied about them. Now he's gotten me in this mess, Boges. Why does he want me out of the way?"

"Come on, we've got no proof of that. I don't think it's Rafe that's gotten you into this mess, I just think he hasn't really helped get you out of it. But think about it, he's had a rough time too. He lost his twin brother. He almost drowned in Treachery Bay. You know, he could have been *killed* at your place that day. And he's got a heart condition, doesn't he? His niece is in a coma. His nephew's on the run from the law. His sister-in-law is on the verge of a nervous breakdown, and he's the only one around trying to keep it all together. Nobody else has stepped up. This can't be easy for him either, Cal. I've seen him at your mum's place, and he looks like a wreck."

"You may be right. He's just so cold all the time, I forget that he may just have a heart in there."

"I don't blame you. Anyway," said Boges, picking up his phone and steering me towards the bathroom where the light was a little brighter, "let's take a quick profile shot. This dump won't give your whereabouts away, but

Web | Images | Video | News | Maps | More ⌄

[   ] **Web Search**

Hello, Callum

Contact Cal
Messages for Cal

Male
15 years old
Richmond

My name is Cal Ormond. I'm 15 and I *used* to go to Richmond High. I'm sure you've heard about me from TV and the papers. Forget it all; nothing they're saying about me is true.
I am innocent.

I love my little sister Gabbi and would never do anything to hurt her. I did not attack my uncle, Rafe. I have no reason to hurt him. I walked into my house last month and found both of them unconscious. I ran to Gabbi and gave her CPR until she was breathing again. I never thought I'd ever have to do CPR for real. I was being chased, so I had to run as soon as the ambulance and police turned up.

Can you imagine finding your little brother or sister unconscious on the floor? It was the worst thing I've ever seen, and lately I've seen a lot. Now she's in a coma and I can't even visit her and tell her it's going to be OK.

Ever since my dad died last year, heaps of bad things have happened to me. My uncle and I nearly drowned in Treachery Bay, because our fishing boat had been sabotaged. Our house was trashed, and then there were the violent attacks on Gabbi and Rafe. My family is being targeted and I don't know why. It's not just the cops that are after me, but it's not safe for me, or my family, if I say any more than that.

Inbox
Update Profile
Sign Out

I'm on the run and everyone thinks I'm the bad guy. I am *not* a dangerous person and I did not hurt my uncle or my sister. Please believe me. I need people on my side. All I want to do is clear my name and stay alive so that I can look after my family. That's all I want. Please, if you know anything at all that might help my case, contact me here before it's too late.

POSTED BY TEENFUGITIVE AT 1:31 PM   0 Messages you'd better turn your face a little," said Boges, "so that most of you is in shadow."

Like my life is now. In the shadows.

Boges pointed the phone at me and took a picture.

"That'll do. I'll upload it all now."

"I hope Mum sees this," I said.

"I'll make sure she does," said Boges.

"Maybe she'll change her mind about me."

Boges nodded, but I could tell he was just being nice.

"The cops will see it, eventually," he said, "but it won't help them. We'll just need to be really careful about where and when we post messages."

Boges started to pack up his gear. "I'll come by again on the weekend," he said. "Oh, and I almost forgot, I bought this for you to keep the drawings in."

He handed me a strong, rigid plastic folder, with a clip seal on one side. "Keep them in this. They're going to fall apart unless they're properly protected."

He paused, and I could see he had something on his mind.

"What?" I asked, taking the folder from him.

"Man," he said, picking up his laptop, "be

careful, OK? I mean it. Don't think you're safe even for a second, because you're not. I hate to say it, but I don't want to add you to the list of tragedies."

"I know. I'm no good to anyone if I'm dead."

"I'm willing to do anything to help. You know that. I think this blog is a good move, but just remember that it's never too late to come in from the cold. I don't want to lose the best buddy a guy ever had. You want to run with it, I'm with you. You want to drop the whole thing, I'm with you too. So ask yourself . . . are you totally sure you want to persist with this? Unraveling your dad's secret? Now that you're starting to realize the full extent of the danger?"

In the dim light of the derelict house, Boges's words sounded ominous, almost frightening: *The full extent of the danger.* I'd made a promise to myself when I was back in my old house, looking into the eyes of my dad in the family photo, and I wasn't going back on it.

"There's no way I can turn back now," I said. "It's what keeps me going."

"Keeps you going? I never picked you for a thrill-seeker," said Boges, unsmiling.

"Far from it. I just know that I'd be no good to anyone in juvenile detention either."

I looked around the dump I was living in. "The only thing I've got going for me is the *truth*. I know it's dangerous, but while there's the chance to solve the mystery of the Ormond Singularity and clear my name, I must do it. I *have* to do it. Otherwise I'm going to be on the run all my life."

7 FEBRUARY

328 days to go . . .

4:03 pm

I'd given up trying to call Winter, convinced that she had given me a dud number. I was beginning to think that she had just been stringing me along with her talk of knowing about the Angel. Who knew whether any of the stories that this girl had spun really happened as she told them?

True to his word, Boges arrived, climbing up through the floor again. I'd been dying to see him, not only just to have some company, but to find out whether my blog had gone live OK.

"It's up and running," Boges assured me, "and you're getting heaps of hits!"

I felt better hearing that. Not quite so cut off from the world. "Has anyone posted anything yet?"

"Not yet, but I think it's just a matter of someone making that first move — people are probably a bit nervous about it. But I reckon once you get that first comment, hundreds will follow. I'll let you know when it happens."

Boges pulled out the little black leather notebook that he carried with him everywhere — it was filled with his middle-of-the-night ideas, complicated sketches and almost indecipherable notes, and was held together by a rubber band.

"'The Ormond Riddle Society is dedicated to the fostering and performance of Tudor and Renaissance music,'" he read. "I've been meaning to tell you about the info I found on the Net about the Ormond Riddle. It's not great — like that was from some singing group's website."

He was right, that wasn't great news.

"Another website explained that the Ormond Riddle," Boges continued, "was thought to have been written by a famous Tudor musician, William Byrd. But there wasn't anything there on the actual words . . . or music . . . or whatever it is we're looking for. I'll search again when I get a chance. In the meantime, can we take another look at the drawings?"

"Sure." I lifted the drawings out from under some loose floorboards, emptied the folder and spread them out on the floor. Boges pointed to the image of the Sphinx, tapping his finger on the pencil drawing of the crouching mythical beast and the Roman guy in front of it.

"I've been reading up on the Sphinx and Egypt," he said, "trying to figure out why your dad might have drawn it. I don't know what *this* drawing means exactly, but I did find out something interesting."

"Yeah?" I prompted. "Spit it out."

"The Sphinx is connected with a riddle."

"A *riddle*?" A charge of energy made me sit up straight. "Now that *is* interesting. The riddle of the Sphinx and the Ormond Riddle."

"Your dad had riddles on the brain, and I bet he knew about the Ormond Riddle. Maybe he even knew the words. Is there anyone else in your family who might know something?"

"Maybe one of my old relatives can help — the

great-uncle or great-aunt. I didn't get out to Great-uncle Bartholomew's as planned, but he's probably my best shot."

I didn't have much family. Dad's parents had died long ago, and Mum's few relatives lived overseas.

"Do you think Dad was trying to suggest that the secret he was on to — the Ormond Singularity — had something to do with solving the Ormond Riddle?"

"Yes, and that's why I've checked the dictionary for exactly what *riddle* means."

"Isn't it kind of like a joke? Some sort of trick?"

"Listen and learn, dude," said Boges, reading from his notebook yet again. "According to the dictionary, a riddle is 'a question or a statement requiring thought to answer or understand; something perplexing, something that requires solving; an enigma.'"

"A what?"

"Yeah, I had to look that one up too. An enigma is something secret or hidden," said Boges.

"We already knew that!" I said in frustration. "Take a look at them. They're *all* enigmas!"

"Hang on a minute. You wouldn't have known

anything about a riddle if you hadn't seen the words 'Ormond Riddle' in your uncle's office. Your dad wasn't to know you'd get that piece of information," he said, getting up and packing up his things.

"I just wish Dad'd told us something a bit more helpful."

"Dude," said Boges, his round face suddenly very serious. "Look what we're up against. Your dad knew he had to be very careful conveying this information to you, and that was before his mind went on him. You're lucky he managed the drawings."

Boges flipped the rubber band back around his notebook and slipped it into his pocket. "Of course, he was also counting on me being here to help you figure it all out. I mean, seriously, what would you do without me?"

"I don't know whether it's your brain or your modesty that I like best about you, Boges."

"I can imagine, dude. It must be tough keeping up with me. And don't think for a second I'm boasting about my talent. It's just a fact."

He was only kidding around, but it was true. At school Boges came first, year after year, in just about every subject. And then of course, there was all his electronic stuff, completely self-taught. He could take any old piece of junk off the street and have it functioning again in no time. He'd once built a robotic backpack on caterpillar treads that "walked" along behind him to school and into the classroom. He'd made and sold quite a few, until the teachers banned them when they realized Boges had really just designed them so he could stage monster-truck-style crashes with the other kids in the corridors.

"Between us," said Boges, "we'll work it out. When I get home from school, I'm going to track down who this Roman is, and do another search for the Ormond Riddle on the Net. I'm also going to see if 'Ormond Angel' takes me anywhere."

"Good idea."

I looked at the strong features of the drawing of the Roman, the way the hair was curled over the guy's forehead, the thick nose and empty eyes. It looked just like one of those marble heads that you'd see in a museum. I thought I understood the Sphinx. But together with the head? It made no sense.

Sirens started wailing out on the street. I jumped up and hurried over to peer through a crack near the door.

I jumped back in fear. "Cops! There are cops

out on the street!"

"Uh-oh, I hope they didn't follow me," whispered Boges. "I was so careful — always am."

He squinted through the crack just as I had done. "There's a police van across the road," he said, turning around. "If they see me coming out of here and someone recognizes me . . ."

"Quick! Under the house," I said, grabbing the drawings and shoving them back into the plastic folder.

Boges jumped first, and then I crawled down after him. This time we carefully made our way to the back of the house and underneath the porch.

Beyond a small clearing directly in front of the porch, the garden had turned into a jungle, and vines had almost completely smothered the bushes and small trees. We forced our way through it to the old back fence.

"Gotta go," said Boges. "Mum'll be wondering where I am — I promised I'd take her shopping. You know what she's like with her English."

"That's cool, but come back soon. You know I can't do this without you."

"Aw, shucks," joked Boges, his round face grinning wide like a Halloween pumpkin. He pressed a twenty-dollar bill into my hand. "And here's me thinking you didn't care!"

I gave him a quick jab, which he returned, then he climbed the fence and disappeared.

7:11 pm

I waited under the house, watching the cops across the road for about an hour. It seemed like there was some kind of domestic dispute over there, and nothing at all to do with me and my hideout.

Back inside, I tried to focus on all the information I had from the drawings so far. We had a collection of things that could be worn, a blackjack, something that seemed to point to the Ormond Riddle . . .

Then of course, there was a certain someone who claimed to know more about the drawings of the Angel.

I had to get more information from her. I had to take a chance.

9 FEBRUARY

326 days to go . . .

Car Lot

9:04 am

With my hoodie pulled down over my face, I risked making my way back to Sligo's car lot. I'd tossed and turned about it for a couple of nights, but I had no choice. I didn't know where else to start looking for Winter, and I had to speak to her. Time was ticking.

I hid behind some bushes across the road from the main entrance, and although I saw people coming and going, including the stocky guy with the red tank top who had tossed me in the tank, I didn't see any sign of her.

It was a much bigger establishment than I'd first realized. Most of it had been in darkness when Sligo had captured me. I'd only seen the office, the laundry area and the closely surrounding lot under lights. Everything between there and running for the gate was a haze. Deeper into the lot there were long lines of cars under tarps and a number of small sheds filled with engine parts and engine blocks.

I was about to leave, after an hour or so of monitoring the place, when a sudden movement caught my eye. Over in the left-hand corner of the yard, near the road, someone was scampering up and over the fence. I sat up, alert. Someone was sneaking into Sligo's car lot! They must have been pinching spare parts! The thief was safe with me — there was no way I'd be running to the boss to tell him about it. I could see the figure more clearly as he quietly made his way further in. It was a kid wearing boots, jeans and a dark brown hoodie, and he seemed to be creeping along the rows of covered cars, looking for something in particular. As he lifted the tarps, one by one, I could see that many of the cars had been in bad crashes, their bumpers crushed, wheels and axles bent at odd angles. I guessed the kid was looking for a part from a specific make and model.

It was an unusual feeling, being the quiet witness for once instead of being the one trying to get on with business without being caught. The kid jumped down from a car not too far from me and when he stood up . . . I saw that he was actually a *she*!

Her slim figure quickly dropped to the ground again and off she went, crawling along the rows of cars, lifting tarps, dropping them and then proceeding to the next wreck.

As I stood up to leave, she must have noticed the movement and swung around to see who was watching her. I was quicker and dropped back down behind my cover, peering once more through the bushes.

The girl frantically scanned the street and then, satisfied that no one was there, she continued with her search.

Slowly, I got to my feet and backed away, completely puzzled.

What on earth was Winter Frey doing creeping around Sligo's car lot?

12 FEBRUARY

323 days to go . . .

Hideout
38 St. Johns Street

12:13 pm

Winter had been on my mind even more since I spotted her at the car lot. What was she doing there, sneaking around? Did she have a little side business of her own — stealing spare parts from Sligo and then selling them elsewhere? I'd wanted to call out to her — I'd gone there to find her — but I knew she would have just run away from me. And she would *not* have been happy about being spotted . . .

I looked at her number in my phone, frustrated that I could never reach her on it. I shoved it back into my bag.

It had been a few days since I'd last seen Boges, and I hadn't been able to get hold of him either.

"Boges!" I said, after practically diving across the room to answer my phone before it stopped ringing.

"I know, I'm sorry, I haven't been able to talk the last couple of days, but anyway, dude, I have some news."

"Has something happened to Mum or Gabbi?" I asked, my chest pounding.

"Gabbi, I'm sorry to say, is much the same," said Boges. "Your mum's fine, but . . ."

"But what?"

"She's moving into Rafe's place."

My heart sank. I knew it was probably going to happen sooner or later, with our house already up for rent, but I'd been hoping some sort of miracle would solve Mum's money problem before any decisions like that'd have to be made.

"I knew you wouldn't be happy about it," said Boges, "but, hey, I checked your blog and it looks good — you've gotten some messages now."

"Really?"

"A few people are having their say about you. Yeah, you've got your regular dose of crazies in there but some are definitely on your side. Well, two at least. Real hotties, Tash and Jasmine."

I felt a smile creep up on my face. Cute names, I thought.

"What did they say?"

"Just that they could tell you weren't a bad guy, and that everyone should be innocent until proven guilty," he said.

I nodded to myself, feeling great that two girls I didn't even know believed in me.

"And then," continued Boges, "they said that they thought you were pretty hot and that they'd like to protect you from the real bad guys . . ."

"What?"

"I'm serious! That's what they said. It's amazing what a life of crime can do for a guy!"

Boges fumbled with the phone for a moment. "If you were here you would see that I've got my hand up, and I'm waiting for a high five. Come on, don't leave me hanging!"

We both cracked up laughing.

"I think it might even be helping *my* popularity," said Boges. "Madeleine Baker sat next to me in Art this morning."

"No way!"

"First she said that she really liked my metal spider sculpture from last year, at least until I designed that program for it and it got away . . ."

"Yeah, right out of the school gates and under a bus!"

"Then Maddy said that it must have been so

hard on me, finding out that my best friend was . . ." Boges hesitated.

"Was what?"

". . . a psycho." I could hear Boges shuffling around uncomfortably. "Sorry, I didn't mean to bring that up. I told her that it didn't bother me a bit — you weren't a psycho, and that it would just be a matter of time before everyone else understood that."

I hated hearing that, but it wasn't surprising. I knew very well what everyone was thinking about me. My own mother thought I was a monster.

"So she ended up sitting somewhere else?" I asked.

"No, she didn't actually. We're now paired up for a photography project. We'll be sitting together whether we want to or not!"

"If you were here you'd see that my hand's up and ready for a high five, Boges. Come on, don't leave me hanging!"

We both laughed again.

I wanted to see the blog comments for myself. Maybe even add some of my own. I decided I'd check it all out at an internet cafe as soon as it was safe.

"I think this whole blog thing is great, but it's also caused a lot of flak," said Boges. "The Police

Commissioner was on the news last night saying that they wouldn't be shutting your page down. They're hoping to trace you. To luck onto information that will lead them to you."

"I'm not going to slip up and give anything away. But can they trace me electronically?"

"It would be very hard to do. I've done a lot of fancy footwork to make it near-impossible."

"You're a legend, Boges. Thanks."

I could hear the distant sound of hundreds of kids fooling around in the schoolyard coming down the phone line.

"I think I've given up on Winter," I said. "Her phone's still turned off."

"Might be just as well," said Boges. "She's part of Sligo's mob. How do you know they're not a team? You know, like playing good cop, bad cop."

"What are you saying?"

"I've been thinking about it. That whole thing in the oil tank could have been a setup. Sligo pretends to try and kill you, then she pretends to save you when all seems lost, so you tell her all your secrets out of gratitude. But all the time she's reporting back to the big guy."

"Boges, I really don't think so. I was seconds away from death when she stopped the oil pump."

"Don't you see?" Boges asked. "That's what they want you to believe. You start to trust her and let your guard down, then you open up, all about the drawings, your dad's letter, the empty jewel case . . . and they add all that to what they already know. It works heaps better than drowning you in sump oil."

I thought about it for a moment. Boges could be right. And I hadn't even told him about spotting her snooping around the car lot.

"But we don't know what they might know already," I said.

"Exactly," said Boges. "And that's why you have to be extra cautious."

There was a sudden sound outside the front of the house. I dropped to the floor. "Gotta go," I whispered. "There's someone outside the house."

The sound came again — a ripping, tearing sound. Someone was wrenching the boards off the front door, trying to get inside!

I shouted down the phone. "Boges, I've gotta go!"

Not caring how much noise I made, I grabbed the folder with the drawings inside and stuffed everything into my backpack, then pushed it through the hole in the floorboards. The sound of splintering wood filled the air.

I took a quick glance around, and hoping I hadn't left any incriminating material lying around, I dove through the hole in the floorboards, twisting to pull the carpet back into position over the opening.

Panting, I crawled under the house, making my way through the dense growth to where Boges had made his escape earlier.

3:19 pm

I drove myself through the jungle of leaves and branches, launched over the back fence, swung myself over into the neighbor's yard, and hit the ground running.

There was yelling and shouting behind me, but I just kept ducking and weaving, putting street after street between me and the St. Johns house.

Deserted railway yard

3:52 pm

I stopped running in the west of the inner city, near the railway. Sweat poured down my body as I squeezed through a fence into a deserted area, where old railway sheds and rusting carriages stood, separated by thick grass growing high between them. I practically collapsed on the ground, hidden under an old carriage, hoping that the intruders had not been the cops.

4:04 pm

It didn't look like the yards had been used in years. I scanned for security cameras. I couldn't see any — there wasn't really anything there to protect from thieves — but I kept my head down anyway.

4:43 pm

When the coast was clear, I crawled out and began investigating the area more closely. Not far from my hiding place there was a deep drain: a cement canal that followed the sloping land. I jumped down into it and followed it until I came to the opening of a huge pipe culvert that must have directed the storm water underground. It was like the opening of a railway tunnel, only a third of the size. It was barred, but the bars had been bent, allowing me to squeeze through them quite easily.

Further in, the cement floor of the tunnel sloped away into darkness. This might be a good place to lay low for a while, I thought. I dug around in my backpack and pulled out my flashlight. The light revealed graffiti-covered walls. Some of the tags I recognized from around the city. There were two that dominated all the others:

WHEN iT RAINS NO DRAINS

no psycho

It hadn't rained in ages, so I didn't have to worry about the first warning. But the second one troubled me. It was one I'd seen a lot of in the last couple of weeks, and I hoped there *was* "no psycho" lurking down in the darkness with me. Me and the rats . . .

I walked on.

5:23 pm

I could no longer see the light from where I'd entered the tunnel behind me, and was surrounded in darkness. I moved my flashlight around and saw that the graffiti and the tagging had thinned out. Obviously not many people were keen to venture this far into the drain.

5:36 pm

I came to an intersection where the storm water drain had widened and split into a Y-shape, now with two drains leading off into more darkness. Just above head height, my flashlight revealed two deep recesses in the walls of the drain, one on each side, possibly for the maintenance workers to store stuff. I shone the flashlight around to check out both of them, deciding that the one on the left looked drier. No one could see me if I was up there and kept up against the wall. I could camp up there. I'd hear people coming — their footsteps would echo loudly down to me — and I'd be able to get out well before they reached me by disappearing down one of the smaller channels.

I threw my backpack up first and carefully placed the flashlight up there to give me light. I got a good grip with my fingers and hauled myself up. The rock climbing I'd done with Dad in the past helped.

I spread myself out on my sleeping bag, ripped open a package of crackers, and started thinking about the people from my blog who, for whatever reason, believed in me.

And I thought of that strange girl, Winter, and wondered again what game she was playing. I hoped Boges was wrong about her.

9:00 pm

I woke up sore and cramped.

I needed to do something. I couldn't just keep moving from hole to hole. I was almost halfway through month number two. I was warned I needed to survive 365 days — how far in was I? My brain was too messy to figure out that simple subtraction.

The bottom line was that this nightmare wasn't going to resolve itself. If Winter wasn't going to help me, the only place I could think of hunting down information was the house I'd escaped from after the first kidnapping.

I needed to know more about my enemies. I'd have to stop being the hunted and instead hunt *them* down.

10:20 pm

Hurrying along the dark roads, I searched for familiar street names, buildings, houses, anything that I recognized from my long run home after escaping from the first kidnapping. I was determined to find that house again, and although I'd only seen a small part of the front entrance, the tiles and the inside of the broom closet, I felt confident that if I saw it again, I'd know it.

But finding the right street — that was another

matter altogether.

10:52 pm

A couple of times I thought I'd seen something familiar, but I wasn't led anywhere. I was looking for a particular intersection that I remembered seeing not long after escaping from the broom closet. It had a small church on one corner, a twenty-four-hour carwash with a couple of pinball machines in it on another, and on the other side was the large, fenced-off area of a school playground.

I felt like I was getting warmer.

11:23 pm

I was thinking about having to face the long walk back to the drains if I hadn't made any progress, when I squinted, straining to see if the little building I was approaching was in fact the church I was looking for.

On the right was a carwash and a schoolyard, dark, empty and eerily lit by the street lights. I hurried closer.

I'd found the intersection!

I stood on the edge of the curb in front of the church and tried to take myself back to that night — I'd been so filled with fear and adrenaline at the time, it was a wonder I remembered anything.

I recalled the distinct sandstone curbing that I'd stumbled on as they'd dragged me, sack slipping from my head, out of the car, and so I began running down the road alongside the church, searching the driveways to find a match. I quickly passed the houses, giving each one a good look, until finally, through the front gates of a large place, I recognized the pavement I'd stumbled on. I jumped back as a car made its way down the street and continued past me.

Quietly, I climbed over the fence, slipped up the driveway and took cover behind some big recycling bins. There was a four-wheel drive parked under a carport. The inside of the house was completely dark. There weren't any lights on. Hopefully, that meant no one was up.

I looked around for any other signs that this was the place I was after, but only found some little kids' bikes leaning up against the carport wall. I crept up and peered into the car. A bruised apple, sunscreen, some baby wipes and a booster seat.

I had to be in the wrong place . . .

13 FEBRUARY

322 days to go . . .

12:08 am

It was now after midnight. I trusted my instincts and decided to move on. Back out on the street, I restarted my search for the sandstone curbing.

Sure enough, a hundred yards or so up the road, I found another sandstone driveway and big, open front gate. I crept up and squatted beside a plumbing van that was parked next door, so I could try and get a better look.

There were soft voices and signs of movement. I strained to pinpoint where they were coming from.

A car door closing. *It was the dark blue Mercedes from the kidnapping!*

Someone fumbling with keys.

A woman's heels clicking on the pavers, followed by dull, heavier footsteps.

Two people — one of them a woman wearing a spotted scarf around her head, and a large man's figure in shadow — were making their way from the car to the front door.

From my vantage point, I watched as they went inside, lights switching on to indicate where in the house they'd moved to.

The house was heavily secured with metal bars over the lower windows and a thick security door at the front. I was feeling pretty sure I'd found the right place, but how was I ever going to get inside?

12:19 am

Beside the house was a very tall pine tree that had recently been lopped. Its lower limbs had been cut back from the driveway near the entrance and almost formed a natural "ladder" that was just asking me to climb it.

12:22 am

The branches scratched my face and hands on the climb up, and the mosquitoes were hammering me too, but I could now see clearly into the house through an open window near the balcony on the second floor.

And there, inside, were the red and black tiles that I'd stood on while I was interrogated by that deranged woman!

The door inside the main room in my view opened and in came two people. The woman had removed her scarf and her crimson-red hair was piled up high in an elaborate hairstyle. Crimson-red! How had I known this without ever seeing her before? I'd barely seen anything but the floor during the abduction and interrogation, and yet, for some reason, I'd remembered her as a woman with red hair . . . the exact woman behind the desk that I was staring at through the pine needles!

She leaned into a drawer and pulled out a long, thin brownish cigarette — a cigarillo. Smoke filled the room and began floating up and out of the window towards me. I held my breath.

She was talking to the man that had accompanied her from the car, who was now standing on the other side of the desk. His suit jacket strained against his bulging body. He looked like a big exercise ball wearing clothes. The redhead's unforgettable voice was loud and distinct, strong and aggressive. She was gesturing with her hands and stabbing the air with the cigarillo as if she were making important points. He too seemed to have a lot to say, and they were both very interested in some papers on the desk in front of her.

From the way she dominated the room and conversation, I knew this was the woman who had questioned me the night I was abducted from Memorial Park. I remembered the way Sligo had reacted when I'd described her to him, the way he'd spat and then ground his heel on the wet spot. He knew very well who she was.

I pulled out my phone, wishing the camera function had a better zoom. Luckily, the room was fairly well lit, so I didn't need my flash. I quickly took the best picture I could of the woman. It wasn't great, but I'd definitely captured her basic shape and features. She was quite a unique character, so I was hoping that someone, somewhere, might recognize her.

Inside, the woman crushed out the cigarillo and opened a tall glass jar on her desk filled with tiny silver balls. She popped a few in her mouth, and I recognized them as being the cachous that Gabbi loved using to decorate cupcakes. She then opened a laptop in front of her. The computer screen radiated bluish light onto her face. I wondered again whether she was the woman who'd first called me claiming to have information on my dad . . . and then set me up. Was she *Jennifer Smith*?

From behind the laptop she suddenly called the big guy over with a dramatic flap of her arms. He rushed to her side and leaned in to see whatever it was on the screen that was so intriguing. They stared at each other for a moment, quite intently, and before I knew it, the redhead had turned and was peering out the window right at me!

12:35 am

I instantly dropped heavily to the ground. My movement must have activated an automatic spotlight — the garden was lit up like a stadium at night. I ran down the driveway and into the darkness. I didn't pause to listen to what was going on behind me. All my energy was focused on getting out of there.

I ran back down the street towards the intersection and then back the way I'd come.

When I'd run far enough and figured it was safe, I stopped to see if anyone was on my trail.

Nothing.

I strained to listen for a car, voices, footsteps . . . Nothing.

No one was chasing me. I was running without a pursuer. Had they seen me? I was sure the woman had looked right at me! Did they have security cameras outside? Was I completely paranoid? Had I fled for no reason?

Whatever the case, I'd found the house, taken a picture of the woman, and made it out of there in one piece.

14 FEBRUARY

321 days to go . . .

Storm water drain

10:10 am

I'd spent a whole day lurking in the drain. Boges wasn't going to manage meeting up with me for another day or two, so I'd tried to keep busy walking up and down the tunnels, rifling through my stuff, sleeping, staring at the ceiling . . . talking to myself.

I had to get out again.

Central Station

11:29 am

Now I was just another anonymous kid wandering the streets near Central Station. Nothing unusual about that. Or so I kept telling myself.

I tried to act calm and cool and remain unnoticed, but I felt like a hundred pairs of eyes were on me.

I stopped by a basketball court where a bunch of kids were having a shoot-out. I'd always liked playing basketball — or any sport, really —and wished I had it in me to go over and play with them.

All of a sudden I felt the hairs on the back of my neck prickling. Someone *was* watching me. I was sure of it. I swung around, but there was no one there. I turned my attention back to the basketball court, and that's when I got the shock of my life!

There was a kid on the other side of the court staring at me through the fence! But that wasn't what had frozen me.

I stared back in disbelief!

Was I seeing things?

He looked as shocked as I did, which didn't help.

My brain tried to make sense of it. Was I looking at some sort of reflection? I rubbed my eyes like some freaked-out cartoon character, but when I looked again, he was still there.

He was the spitting image of me — or, at least, what used to be me. My face, my body, my eyes, my nose, my jaw, my eyebrows. *My* face!

My face before I had to try and make myself unrecognizable.

I stared again. He still looked just like me, and he was still staring right back at me.

I was spellbound.

I finally snapped myself out of it and shouted to him.

"Hey!" I yelled, as I started to run around the side of the court, trying to get to him. The moment I started running, so did he. But he was running *away* from me.

He took off, legs and arms pumping, like he was running for his life. It was like some bizarre, out-of-body experience, like seeing *me* running for *my* life a month ago.

"Hey! Wait!" I called after him.

But he wouldn't look back. He just kept running. I kept on after him, watching him try to duck and weave and lose me in the crowds, through narrow alleys and one-way streets. They were all the tricks I'd come to know so well.

I was able to keep him in sight, almost all the way down to the harbor, but that's where I lost him.

It was hopeless. I just couldn't keep up. My body was completely worn out. And he was fast — as fast as I used to be.

I stopped, doubled over, trying to catch my breath, and trying desperately to make sense of what I'd just seen.

15 FEBRUARY

320 days to go . . .

Internet cafe

11:11 am

I took a seat right at the back, choosing a computer with its screen facing the back wall, away from prying eyes, although the place was practically empty.

I went straight to my blog. My shadowed profile pic' appeared, and I was reminded of the kid I'd seen at the courts yesterday. I was going crazy trying to figure out why there was this guy running around the city who looked exactly the same as me. He must have been asking himself the exact same question.

But I couldn't waste any more time on that mystery just now — I had other important things to do.

I had a lot of messages on my wall. Some of it was horrible — complete strangers calling me all sorts of names. Some were from people who said

Web | Images | Video | News | Maps | More ▾

Web Search

Hello, Callum

Contact Cal
Messages for Cal

Male
15 years old
Richmond

| Write on Callum's Wall | Messages for Cal |

14.02
J@s &T@sh:
U rock! We believe in u ☺. Oh, and
Happy Valentine's Day!!
Luv Jasmine and Natasha xo

they wanted to join my gang.

Like I was some sort of street gangster.
Yesterday was Valentine's Day? I hadn't even
noticed. At least it meant that I'd made it
through the first half of the month.

"You're checking up on the psycho kid, are ya?"

Startled, I turned around towards the voice
that had interrupted me. It was the man who ran
the place — a tall, lanky guy in his mid-forties.
He must have been bored with the quiet day. I
couldn't blame him, but I wasn't up for small
talk. I hit the "close" button fast.

"Hey, I was just reading that," he said.

"Oh, sorry, I have to get going," I mumbled.

"He's got some nerve putting himself up on the web like that," the guy continued. "I read somewhere that psychopaths will do anything for attention. But boy, that kid must be an animal. Imagine your own brother doing that to you." He shook his head and then flicked a dead fly away from the keyboard beside me. "No wonder his mum's lost her mind."

He looked down at me and frowned. "You come in here a bit, don't you?"

"Yeah, you've probably seen me here before," I lied. "I'm waiting for my dad to get my laptop fixed." I turned back to face the screen and reached down to grab my bag. I hadn't been in there before. I had to get out of there before he figured out why I looked familiar.

"You kids these days, you have it too easy. Gadgets, cell phones, chat rooms, all kinds of information you can download in seconds, fancy cars the minute you can drive. You don't have to work for anything," he said, looking around at his empty seats and idle screens. "Not like I had to. Too easy. You kids don't know anything about how hard life really is."

Try living in a drain, pal, I longed to say.

"You're probably right," I said instead. And with that, I got up and left.

16 FEBRUARY

319 days to go . . .

Burger Barn

12:05 pm

Boges and I were meeting in a busy, noisy fast food place. We'd decided that'd be safer than the drain, where two people caught lurking would surely mean questions and, ultimately, trouble.

Plus, I was thinking that making Boges come to the St. Johns dump was bad enough. I really didn't want him to see my latest living quarters.

I'd noticed the man from the internet cafe who'd spoken to me yesterday, but I kept my head turned as he passed.

Boges appeared, pulled out the other chair and plonked his tray down on the table. "So what ya got for *me*?" he asked, as he unloaded a couple of burgers, some chips and two drinks.

"I saw this guy who looks exactly like me," I said in a rush. I waited for him to sit down, then I leaned in closer. "I mean *exactly* like me. He was staring at me through the fence down at the Central Station basketball courts, and then as soon as I tried to talk to him, he bolted."

"I don't blame him," said Boges. "If I didn't know you, I'd run, too. Dude, you look feral."

I looked past my friend's head and shoulders to the frosted glass behind him, where I could see my reflection. I had to admit that I did look like the sort of guy that any normal person would run away from.

"But Boges," I persisted, "I'm telling you, he was the spitting image of me. Exactly. The. Same," I said slowly, to push the point. "And he was staring at me, like he knew me, or like he was wondering what I was wondering — why is there a guy in front of me who looks exactly the same as me?"

"You mean he had a bad fake tat on his neck, a bunch of piercings and hair like a rat's nest?"

"No."

"So he *didn't* look exactly like you."

"He looked exactly like I *used* to look," I said impatiently. "It was crazy. I was completely freaked out. We both were."

Boges took a huge mouthful of his burger. "You know that they say that everyone has a double — a *doppelganger* — and it's not a good sign if you run into yours . . ."

"What do you mean?"

"Let's just say it means bad news. Maybe it's just another of the mysteries of the city. I've been working on one of them — the DMO —"

"The what?" I asked.

"The DMO," he repeated, pronouncing it like *Dee-mo*. "The Dangerous Mystery of the Ormonds." Boges grinned. "I found out more about the riddle of the Sphinx — it's connected to a different sphinx than the one your dad drew."

The only one I knew of was the one he'd drawn — the Great Sphinx of Giza, in Egypt.

"This other sphinx is very different," Boges continued, "she was some kind of psycho woman who was half lion. She had attitude — the sort of sphinx who stopped people passing by and asked them to solve a riddle, and if they didn't get it right, she'd kill them. Strangle and devour them."

"OK, so what about the Roman guy? Where do you think he fits in?"

Boges shrugged. "I'm still working on that. In History I asked Mr. Addicot about whether there were any Roman connections with the Sphinx, and apparently Julius Caesar was involved in some business in Egypt around 48 BC."

"This is the *Egyptian* Sphinx you're talking about now, right? Not cat woman?"

"Right. We've got to keep in mind that the drawings don't actually mean exactly what's in them — we've gotta learn how to think like your dad did. Sort of diagonally. Sideways thinking." Boges demonstrated his point with his hands. "So, here's what I reckon he was trying to tell us. This huge secret he was in the process of uncovering is something to do with *history*, a life and death riddle, and someone in power — a king or a ruler, someone like Julius Caesar." He sat back. "And then there's also something to do with a jewel — something you wear — that may or may not have been stolen from your dad's suitcase, and a blackjack . . . or a 21. It's a bit lame, but it's the best I can do right now."

I threw a chip at him. "Someone in power. That really narrows it down. There's only been about a trillion kings and rulers in history."

Boges picked the chip off his shirt and ate it. "It could also just mean that your dad was stressing that discovering the truth about the Ormond Singularity was really important."

"That part I do get," I said, thinking again of the demented guy yelling out his warning on that hot December afternoon when it all began.

I sighed. Dad was certainly hiding things well. Putting the "M" into the DMO.

"The only other thing we can do at this stage," said Boges, "is call that Eric guy from your dad's work and see if he knows anything at all about this from his time in Ireland — without giving too much away, of course."

I took another bite of my fast-diminishing hamburger. "Yep, I'll do that as soon as I can. Any luck on the words of the Ormond Riddle?"

"No, nothing's showing up."

Nothing was making enough sense to me to matter. And I couldn't stop thinking about my double. It wasn't a surprise that it meant bad news.

"So what else has been happening?" I asked. "Anything from school? Any special valentines from Maddy?"

"No," Boges laughed. "Maybe next year . . . You never know. All the guys at school are wondering where you are, and what's happened to you. They're always asking me."

It felt weird to know that everyone was talking about me.

"Mr. Addicot asked me more about you, too," said Boges, "like trying to figure out whether I knew anything about your whereabouts. I just played dumb." Boges grinned. "Believe me, my friend, playing dumb was hard. Very hard. Especially when I've been busting my brain applying for a scholarship to the robotics lab at the University of Pennsylvania."

"Pennsylvania, USA?"

"Uh-huh. Their research lab's been awarded millions of dollars in grants to develop robotic cockroaches."

I gave him a kick under the table. "Weren't the cockroaches at my place good enough for you?"

"Hey!" He kicked me back.

Boges had finished eating his hamburger and was eyeing mine. "Hands off!" I ordered. I pulled out my cell phone and found the picture of the redhead I'd taken when I was perched up the tree.

"This is who grabbed me off the street that night near Memorial Park," I said. "I tracked down the house they took me to. Somehow, we have to find out who she is."

Boges snatched the phone from me, his expression startled. "How did you take this?"

"Through an open window. I was up a tree at the time. I tried to zoom in as much as I could, but you know, this phone isn't that great. And anyway," I said impatiently, "who is it? You know her?"

"This chick was on the news last night. I'm sure of it."

"So who is she?" I asked, hoping to find out

how I seemed to recognize her without actually seeing her.

"You're up in a tree, taking photos of this woman through a window, while I'm watching the exact same person on TV? Man that is *weird!*"

TV? I was starting to get annoyed at Boges stringing me along, and I was about to tell him so when he finally said, "This woman is none other than Oriana de la Force, 'the flame-haired leading criminal lawyer in the city,' as the journalist on the news described her . . ."

Criminal lawyer?

"Is *this* the woman you think abducted you?"

"You really know who it is?"

He rolled his eyes at me. "I'm about ninety-nine percent sure it's the same woman. I was watching this show last night, and the journalist said that Oriana — this woman," he said, shoving her picture in my face, "is notorious for taking on difficult and dangerous clients."

I must have recognized her distinct voice from seeing her on the news myself! "*She's* difficult and dangerous!" I said, with a half laugh, thinking about the way she pushed me around and screamed at me the night I was abducted.

"I saw it on TV last night — a current affairs program," continued Boges. "But anyway, that wasn't the first time I'd heard of her. Cal, anyone who takes an interest in what's happening in the world, or at least in the city, would know about her."

It was true I didn't pay too much attention to the news, although being on the run had changed that. Being part *of* the news, making headlines, had forced me to take an interest.

"But why would a leading criminal lawyer become involved in a kidnapping?"

"If you were going to commit a major crime, being a criminal lawyer would have to be a huge advantage, right?"

"I guess it wouldn't be the first time a *criminal* lawyer has given a new meaning to their title," I added.

"Exactly, and a criminal lawyer would know all the traps, and Oriana would know better than anyone how to avoid them. So either she saw your photograph in the newspaper and wanted to adopt a lovely teen male just like you –"

I glared at him.

"Or," he continued, "she herself, or a client of hers, is also after the Ormond secret. The DMO!"

Oriana de la Force had made it very clear that the fortune Dad had hinted at in his letter to me was partly known to her. Too many people knew about it. Had he given too much away when he delivered his paper at the conference? The dangerous mystery of the Ormonds . . . How was I supposed to compete against a brilliant lawyer like Oriana — a lawyer who would easily toss a kid off a cliff? And how could I stay alive when a criminal like Sligo, with all his wealth and underground connections, wanted me dead? I was just an ordinary kid! Well, maybe not ordinary any more — but how was *I* going to win against these people? Luckily, Oriana, at least, figured it was better to keep me alive. But for how long?

"You know," said Boges, "I've never heard of anyone who's had so many people after him — the cops, the infamous king of the underworld, a leading criminal lawyer — plus, and I know you hate hearing it, your own family think you're some kind of monster. It's messed up."

I looked up from checking the time on my phone to see Boges's eyes huge in his frozen face. "Don't move," he hissed, through gritted teeth. "Don't even think about turning around."

Without moving his lips, Boges muttered, "Your uncle and some other dude just sat down at the table behind you. Whatever you do, don't turn around."

Rafe?! Frantic, I tried to think of a way

through this. If Rafe spotted me, I was gone. Every instinct was saying *run*! I hunched down, trying to shrink.

Boges had also hunched down, hand to his head, as if he was thinking deeply. If Rafe spotted *him*, I'd be next. I slid down further in my seat.

The two men behind me were deep in conversation.

"I've given the matter a lot of thought," I heard my uncle's voice behind me, barely above a whisper. "It'll give her a sense of security that she won't have while the house is still in my name."

"Have you thought about the implications of this?" asked the other man. "How are you going to protect your own interests?"

"It's Win's interests I'm thinking of."

Win's interests. Rafe was talking about my mum!

"If she knew she had the house in her name, it would be a great load off her mind. She's already got a daughter in intensive care, and a son . . . well, that kid hasn't had it easy, but the less said about him the better. She's in a terrible way. I'm willing to do anything to help her."

"But signing over the house," protested the other man, "that's being too generous. You're forgetting your own interests — your own security."

"Listen, I can't expect you to understand. This is my brother's wife, *Tom's* wife and family we're talking about. They're all I have. They're all I care about. I feel I have to do it."

"I can tell you've made up your mind, Rafe. Very well. Come to my office tomorrow and we'll do the paperwork."

"I know Tom would have done the same for me. I mean, if I'd been in a similar situation." There was a pause. "This coffee is undrinkable," he added.

A moment later, I heard the scrape of the men's chairs as they got up and left.

I let out a huge breath. I hadn't dared to breathe during that conversation. My mind was spinning. Rafe was signing over his mansion to my mum? I felt a mixed-up rush of gratitude and guilt.

"That was way too close! Did you hear all that?" I asked Boges, when I could speak again.

He nodded. "See? You've been way too hard on him, dude. His heart's in the right place. He's just got a seriously messed up way of showing it."

"You were right," I said, almost numb with shock.

Boges sat across from me, scratching his head like he was trying to put all the paranoid pieces together.

He looked at me, waiting for me to say something.

"I think," continued Boges, "he's been trying to hold everything together — to deal with everything alone."

Just like me, I thought.

Storm water drain

4:46 pm

There was no one around as I slipped through the fence near the railway yards and made my way back towards the big storm water culvert. The crickets stopped their chirping as I snuck past them in the long grass.

My mind was still whirling from seeing Rafe earlier. I felt such confusion and guilt in my stomach.

I hurried down the sloping drain. I'd sleep here for a few more nights, I thought, and then go back to check out the St. Johns house.

18 FEBRUARY

317 days to go . . .

10:32 am

I sat up in the alcove in the drain, the drawings spread around while I stared at them by flashlight. I was trying to figure out what the half-woman, half-lion sphinx might have meant. Had my dad been trying to warn me again about the dangerous woman he mentioned in his letter? The beastly, answer-demanding Oriana de la Force?

The sounds of the city echoed through the drain, and my mind began replaying the moment I'd turned and seen my double staring at me. Had he seen something in me that scared him? Maybe he knew that seeing your doppelganger meant doom.

19 FEBRUARY

316 days to go . . .

Kendall Cove

8:07 am

I'd risked going for a swim off a rocky cove not far from Dolphin Point, a spot where people rarely swam because of the strong currents that often whirled around there. When I first dove into the water it was pretty calm. It felt so good and refreshing to be underwater and free, but I could also feel that the ocean was growing rougher by the minute.

It was a stinking hot day, and as I floated on my back and looked up at the sky, I saw that in the southwest, thunder heads were building — huge gray cauliflowers of cloud with ominous, flattened tops. Time to go.

I climbed up the rocks and hurried to my backpack, secured in a cave-like hole well above the high water mark.

I moved as fast as I could, knowing that I needed to get back to the storm water drain to grab my stuff before the downpour.

Just as the first heavy drops started to hit the hot black tar of the roads, I made it to the tunnel. The roads hissed, and steam lifted like ghosts. It was going to be one of those storms that dumps an inch on the city in half an hour.

Storm water drain

10:53 am

I climbed up into the alcove and took out the plastic folder with Dad's drawings. I forced my sleeping bag into my backpack and wondered how I could best stow the drawings. I was thinking that maybe I should secure the folder on the outside of the backpack with a bungee cord, when I heard voices echoing through the drain.

I grabbed my flashlight and jumped down from my alcove — my backpack and the drawings in one hand, flashlight in the other.

Now the voices were loud — there was a roughness and a nasty edge that I knew meant trouble. One guy in particular had a very ugly laugh. I hesitated, wondering for a moment whether I should try to leave by the main drain, running straight into them, or avoid them by going down one of the smaller tunnels.

It was too late. Three guys appeared, emerging from the main drain into the small clearing before the other two channels branched off. They looked surprised to see me. Their surprise quickly turned to aggression.

"What are you doing here?" asked the leader, a tall guy with black hair slicked back, a scar running through his left eyebrow, and what looked like a permanent sneer on his narrow lips.

"Yeah, we rule the drains. Who do you think *you* are?" The other two echoed from each side of their slick leader. Generally rats ruled the drains, but I thought it wouldn't be a good idea to say that.

The other two guys were smaller than the first. The shorter, stout kid, was dressed in military-style gear, while the other guy had a shaved head and was squeezed into tight black jeans and a striped tank top, like some sort of urban pirate. They stood there snarling at me, while my mind raced for a way to deal with this.

I knew this scenario too well. I'd faced it plenty of times in the schoolyard. A gang of guys looking for a fight. A fight that they can't lose — three against one.

"What's in that bag?" demanded the sneerer, making a lunge for my backpack. I jumped back quickly, out of his reach.

"And what's in the folder? Give it here!"

I knew this game, too. If I didn't give them what they wanted, they'd jump me and grab it anyway. If I *did* give them what they wanted, they'd jump me just the same. You can't always talk sense to bullies, Dad once told me.

"Give me that!" barked Scarface.

"No way," I said, taking a step back, putting more distance between me and them, so I'd have more room to move.

"You'd better," said the guy with the shaved head, taking a step towards me.

"Why don't you come here and get it?!" I said, playing for time, my mind working furiously for a strategy. I needed to deal with the leader first. If I could get him down fast, the other two wouldn't be too hard to take care of. I heard Dad's voice in my head: *Watch their hands, and you'll see the punch coming before it lands.*

"Come on," I taunted, "if you want it so bad, come and get it!"

I glared hard at Scarface, keeping his hands in my peripheral vision. I wasn't feeling anywhere near as tough as I sounded, but there was no way

I was giving my backpack to these losers.

The threesome looked surprised at my attitude, and Scarface's neck and face flushed red, his hands moving fast into furious fists. I braced myself, muscles surging with adrenaline.

He swung at me, and before he knew what hit him, I'd doubled over and charged my head into his gut like a battering ram. I heard him grunt as he went flying backwards, hitting the deck hard.

I kept going, avoiding his flailing arms and legs as he scrambled to recover his balance and his wind. But I was already gone, leaving them all behind me, racing away towards the Y-intersection.

I threw myself into the left-hand branch.

Scarface's swearing and the shouted threats of the others thundered down the drains.

This drain was smaller and more sloped than the main one. As my feet pounded along, the enraged footsteps of the three in pursuit pounded even louder.

"C'mon! Dogs! Freddy! Get the little scumbag!" Scarface yelled to the other two.

I had no idea where I was heading. They were gaining, but I could hear something else — a sound I couldn't identify. It wasn't the distant rumble of trains. It was something else.

I kept running. I was passing dark entrances to other, much smaller drains on my left and right, but they were too small to climb into. Water was starting to trickle from these small drains onto the floor of the one I was running through. I knew that a city the size of mine would have miles of drains beneath it, but I hadn't realized just how extensive this underworld was.

Soon I was splashing through ankle-deep water. But still the footsteps behind me persisted.

The rumbling was getting louder, and I suddenly understood what it was. It was the accumulating sound of dozens of drains rattling under the surge of the water that was pouring down from the city's gutters! Smaller channels were emptying their contents into larger ones, and the larger channels in turn were sending cascades of water into the huge culvert system.

The water was now halfway up my calves, and it was getting harder to run. The guys after me were finding it harder, too.

I was starting to worry. *Give up, you morons!* We all needed to get out of the drain. I remembered Dad telling me that fast-running water, once it gets over your knees, is far more dangerous than it seems.

The drain was becoming steeper, sloping down

towards someplace I didn't even know.

Even the strongest swimmer would find it hard to do battle with the combined tide of the thousands of tons of water that were descending on the roads, sidewalks, and freeways of the city. I was struggling to stay in control. The sound of rushing water echoed loudly throughout the drain, and I couldn't tell whether I was being chased anymore. All I could hear was the roar of the rising water.

Now I was in big trouble, being bumped along by the powerful surge of the fast-flowing water. It knocked me off my feet, and I struggled to hold the folder with Dad's drawings and the flashlight up over my head to keep them dry. When a huge surge of water suddenly hit me, I lost my balance completely, and both the flashlight and the folder flew out of my hands.

As soon as the flashlight hit the water it went out, throwing me into total darkness. I yelled and struck out in the rising drain water, which carried me along like a bodysurfer. I blindly stretched out my arms and fingers, desperate to find the plastic folder. I was only thinking about the drawings.

The power of the surge was pushing me along faster than I could ever swim. It bumped and crashed me against the walls. I had no idea where the drawings were. I was screaming in the dark, hurtling along, shouting for help, but there was no one to hear me.

Ahead of me I thought I could see bluish light.

The light was getting stronger. Now I could see an opening, a grille, above the chop of the ocean. The drawings were lost. By now they'd be somewhere off the coast, sinking to the bottom of the sea. And I could be joining them at any moment.

The surge pushed me faster and faster towards the grille and the ocean. But then I saw something that I could scarcely believe. In front of the grille was a mesh screen, catching plastic and trash. And slap bang right in the middle was the folder! I crashed into it and grabbed the folder. The mesh screen busted out on impact with my body and flew down to the seething ocean below. I hung onto the sides of the grille with one hand, the folder in my other, while the gushing water tried to tear me down.

I clung there for a long time, my head barely above water, my fingers turning wrinkled and white, but I didn't let go of that grille or the folder.

After what felt like an eternity, the water began to subside. Eventually, the water level dropped completely, putting my feet back onto the hard ground.

1:50 pm

Everything was soaked. The gang of three was long gone. I'd made my way back out of the drain and was now walking along unnoticed in the rain — just another drenched pedestrian, sodden and dripping.

I called Boges from a pay phone, and he quickly came to my rescue . . . again. I don't know how, but he managed to fix my damaged phone and flashlight, and he gave me some dry clothes and a waterproof bag to store things more safely.

After about ten minutes he had to go again. If only I could have followed him.

5:33 pm

The alcove in the drain was saturated. Puddles sat where I'd been sleeping — clearly it had not escaped the storm water level. I tried to sweep it out with my wet clothes, so I could rest up for a bit, but I knew I couldn't stay much longer anyway and risk being trapped.

9:01 pm

I settled down, trying to sleep. My body and mind were still churning over the gang I'd faced and the flooding storm. I hated fighting.

Back in our first year at school, one day

Boges and I were about to have our lunch on the benches under the trees when two big kids — Kyle Stubbs and Noah Smith — approached us.

"What's that stuff you're eating, weirdo?" Kyle asked, pointing at Boges's lunchbox.

"Yeah, weirdo." echoed Noah.

Mrs. Michalko had packed Boges fried potato dumplings. She'd put in extra because she knew I loved them too.

Even at six, Boges was reasonable and logical. "It's called *piroshki*, and you're the weirdo, not me."

Kyle kicked Boges's lunchbox, sending the potato dumplings flying out everywhere.

They rolled and coated themselves in playground dust and grass.

"What'd you do that for?" asked Boges. "What am I supposed to have for lunch now?"

"Oh, boohoo," mocked Noah.

I looked around for a teacher, but there was no one in sight.

Kyle kicked at some of the piroshki on the ground. "You can still eat this," he said, with an ugly grin.

With his grubby hands, he scooped up some of the dirty potato dumplings. "Come on, open your mouth!"

Noah grabbed Boges and tried to pry his

mouth open. Boges kicked and struggled, almost falling off the bench. I didn't know what to do. I was so much smaller than these guys. But when I saw Kyle trying to squash the dirt-encrusted piroshki into Boges's mouth, something like fire raced through my body. With all my strength, I flew off the bench where I'd been sitting and rammed Kyle Stubbs. I was only small, and Kyle was huge, but he went flying, knocking Noah to the ground with him in the process.

"Come on, Boges!" I yelled, swinging around and yanking my friend up.

As Kyle and Noah tried to get back to their feet, we raced past them, kicking dirt into their faces.

They never bothered us again.

20 FEBRUARY

315 days to go . . .

10:31 am

"Can I please speak to Eric Blair?" I asked. I'd finally decided to call Dad's work to find out if Eric knew anything.

"I'm sorry," replied the woman on the other end of the line, "Eric Blair's on sick leave. He's . . . he's not well. I can take a message for you, but I'm afraid I'm not sure when he'll be returning to the office."

"That's OK, I'll call back another time," I said, hanging up.

Right away my phone rang, taking me by surprise.

"Hello?"

"Why haven't you called me?"

"Winter?"

"Who else would it be? What's the deal? Why

the silence?"

"What? I've been trying to call you — I tried you heaps. Your phone's been turned off for two weeks!" I started thinking how desperate I must have sounded and started to tone it down. "Whatever."

"Sometimes I'm hard to catch. There are things I have to do. Now, do you want to see that angel or not?"

Swann Street

11:29 pm

As I waited for Winter near the Swann Street station entrance, I looked over a community bulletin board at ads for part-time work, roommates, sales of laptops, cars and furniture. I moved further into the shadows when I saw some "no psycho" tags next to a curling wanted poster with the face I once had on it.

Everyone seemed to want a piece of me.

I patted my backpack, checking to make sure the drawings were safe. I'd slipped the folder underneath the plastic backing of my bag, and unless someone did a really serious search, the drawings couldn't be seen.

WANTED
CALLUM ORMOND

Have you seen this youth?

DESCRIPTION

Age: 15 yrs old   Hair: Blond
Height: 5' 10"   Eyes: Blue-green
Weight: 165 lbs.   Complexion: Medium

If you have any information regarding the
whereabouts of this wanted person, please
contact Police Crime Force Unit #5, immediately.

CAUTION
Do not approach. Suspect is considered armed
and dangerous.

11:35 pm

I spotted Winter before she saw me. In her drifty
clothes, with the light of traffic headlights behind
her, she seemed like some strange being from a

spirit world. As she walked closer I could hear the faint chiming of the tiny silver bells that lined the bottom of her long, white skirt.

To my surprise, she kept on walking past me.

"You wanna see the Angel, don't you?" she asked, turning back, raising one eyebrow.

I looked into her dark, almond-shaped eyes, and she gave me one of her cool smiles.

"I could have waited until tomorrow," I said, "but you insisted it had to be tonight."

"That's right. I'm busy tomorrow."

"School?" I asked.

She shook her head. "I don't go to school. I'm home-schooled. But it still had to be tonight. There's a full moon. I need that."

"Are you planning on turning into a werewolf?" I joked.

"You'll see. Well, come on!"

Although I was joking about the werewolf thing, I realized as I followed her that I had no idea what she was up to. Boges's words of warning were all I could think of. Good cop, bad cop.

11:48 pm

I hurried along to keep up with her as she led me through the city streets, her wild hair trailing behind her. She walked like someone in charge of the world.

It wasn't until we came to the bottom of a hill that I recognized the street leading off to Memorial Park. The park I was abducted from.

"Where are we going?" I asked.

"You'll see."

"I'm the sort of guy who likes to know where he's going."

"Are you now?" She paused. "I thought you wanted to see the Angel."

"I do. I just wanna know where he is already."

"Look, we'll get there quicker if you quit the questions."

Memorial Park

11:52 pm

Last time I was here I ended up in a car's trunk and then locked in a closet. I hung back.

"Come *on!*" Winter grabbed my arm. "You're not afraid, are you?"

"Of course not," I lied.

"Then come on. We're nearly there."

She hurried along in the moonlight, silver bells ringing on her skirt. I tried to stay cool but alert.

11:59 pm

I kept looking around me, checking out every movement in the shadows. In this dark and secluded place, anyone could ambush us — or *me*. My heart jumped at the thought, and a sickening feeling in the pit of my stomach made it hard to concentrate. I was braced, ready for anything. To run like the wind or fight for my life.

We stopped at the low, wide steps at the front of the cenotaph. I'd never been this far into the park before.

"Sometimes the homeless sleep in here," Winter said, dragging open the rusted iron gates that had once closed off the central area of the memorial. The lock looked like it had long since flaked away.

Just before going in, she turned and held out the watch on her wrist. "See?" she joked. "It's almost midnight, there's a full moon, and I haven't turned into a werewolf." She laughed and bared her teeth. "Not yet, anyway."

We stepped over scattered trash and leaves, and I tried to relax as she took my hand and led me further into the moonlit interior.

21 FEBRUARY

314 days to go . . .

Cenotaph
Memorial Park

12:01 am

I found myself in the middle of a wide, circular space with an ornate mosaic floor. Ahead of me, a figure stood on a tall stone pedestal — the sort of statue you see on graves or memorials. It was almost like being back at Crookwood Cemetery, when Boges and I were looking for the Ormond mausoleum at midnight.

It had been a warm, summer night, but now a cold wind had blown in, lifting the dead leaves, making them skitter in an eerie little whirl. I shivered, then looked up at the ghostly statue.

"That's not an angel, it's just a soldier!" Fear gripped me tighter. I was trapped. I'd followed her willingly into this creepy joint and now anyone could grab me, or the drawings.

I was about to hurry back down the steps when she called out to me.

"Where are you going? Look up!"

She held out her arms and looked to the sky. "There's your Angel!"

I hesitated a moment, then did as she said. I lifted my eyes until I was looking right over the statue's head at the stained glass window high up on the wall of the cenotaph. I gasped. There, lit by the light of the moon shining through the colored glass, glowed the huge figure of the Angel *exactly as my father had drawn him*! His gas mask slung around his neck and his tin helmet on his head. Behind him were his outspread wings.

I was stunned. I had found the Angel.

I don't know how long I stared at him. It wasn't until I lowered my gaze and found an inscription at the bottom of the figure that I realized why Dad had drawn this Angel twice —

SACRED TO THE MEMORY
OF PIERS ORMOND,
KILLED IN FLANDERS, 1918

first in his letter to me from Ireland, and again from the hospital bed.

"Ormond." I finally spoke. "That's my surname." I turned to the girl beside me.

"I know that. And yet you didn't know about this memorial?"

"I had no idea," I said, pointing to the stained glass window. "Dad told me ages ago that a relative had died in the Great War, but that didn't really mean anything much to me. I think he must've found something out about it when he was in Ireland and –" I stopped myself in my tracks, realizing I'd been on the verge of telling her about Dad's last letter from Ireland, where he'd begun explaining the massive discovery he was in the process of uncovering.

"And?"

She frowned, realizing I'd stopped myself for a reason. "It's not a very common name," she said. "He could be a relative of yours."

What did it mean? Why had Dad drawn Piers Ormond? How did Winter know about it? My excitement quickly changed to suspicion. "So how do you know about this Angel? Where did you find out about him? Did Sligo tell you?"

"Sligo?" Winter repeated. "Why would you think that? *He* doesn't know about this. *He's* never been here." She gestured towards the Angel. "This is where I come to get *away* from people like Sligo. Stop worrying, Cal. Your angel secret is safe with me."

"What do you mean, *secret*? Why are you saying that? Why do you think there's some secret connected to the Angel?"

In the moonlight, I saw her roll her eyes.

"Oh man. Does being dumb come easy to you, or do you really have to work at it? Of course there's a secret about the Angel! Why else would you be so desperate to find out more? Why else would you be carrying drawings of this very Angel around with you? Why would Sligo be chasing something called the *Ormond* Singularity? Of course there's a secret! You must think *I'm* stupid! Is that it?!"

She was right. It wouldn't have taken a genius to figure it out.

"I think you're a lot of things," I said finally, thinking that she was beautiful, strange, secretive, mysterious . . . and downright irritating, "but *stupid* isn't one of them."

She flashed a look at me. Now *she* was wary, unsure whether my answer was meant as a compliment or an insult. After a pause she spoke again. "I've known about this Angel almost as long as I can remember. I used to come here when I was little. When we were living in Dolphin Point. And then after the accident I came back here a lot."

"The accident," I asked, "when you lost your parents?"

She didn't answer me. I knew she'd lost them in an accident, but what happened? I knew it was probably still far too soon for her to reveal that to me, if ever. She turned away to look up at the Angel again. "Yeah, I used to come here all the time. This was my special spot. It's cool in here in the hot weather, and during the day it's mostly deserted. I still like to sit here sometimes, especially when I'm sad."

If I hadn't seen the sadness on her face when she showed me the photographs of her parents in her locket, I would have said that Winter Frey was way too cool for sad.

Too cool and too tough.

I started to feel that just maybe I could trust her. Was she telling the truth? I had no way of knowing. I put Boges's warnings to the back of my mind and tried to enjoy the moment. This Angel finally connected the Ormond name with two of my dad's drawings, and to the Ormond Riddle. This stained glass window with its information about Piers Ormond was a huge piece of the puzzle Boges and I were trying to put together. I whipped out my phone, took a picture and sent it to Boges.

It suddenly darkened. A cloud must have hidden the moon. I turned around to thank Winter for showing me the Angel. But she was nowhere to be seen. While I was photographing the Angel and sending it to Boges, she'd slipped away.

I could only hope she wasn't running straight to Sligo.

12:34 am

Liberty Square was quiet now. There were only a few people still on the streets. I was striding fast, my hood and collar pulled up around my face. I wanted to go back to St. Johns Street to check out the derelict house. I couldn't go back to sleep in the storm water drain. Not tonight.

Hideout
38 St. Johns Street

1:30 am

I'd crawled under the house but stopped when I heard voices and someone moving around.

I crept up to the porch and snuck around the

side of the house so I could peer through a crack in a boarded up window.

Three people sat around drinking on the floor, the floor that I had spent so many hard nights on. Two men in shabby clothes and a younger woman with a gaunt face and stringy hair were sitting on my chairs, at my table. It was a hot night, but the woman was wearing long black mittens and had an old, woolen shawl draped around her shoulders. They'd been through some of my food — there were empty cans rolling around. I didn't dare interrupt. I didn't want to stir up trouble. But I was really hungry, and when I checked my pockets for money, I found I had hardly anything left of the money Boges had last given me.

I would have to find somewhere else to sleep.

2:01 am

I walked on, head down, and passed a loud group of people eating in one of those cozy twenty-four-hour cafes. I was so hungry. I wondered for a moment how they'd react if I just walked on up to their table, sat down and started nodding and laughing along with them while helping myself to a big handful of their chips.

I was sure it wouldn't go down well.

And how would the waiter react if I sat by the table next to them and started reading the menu?

I knew that wouldn't go down well either. The problem wasn't just that I didn't have enough money. I looked like a mess. I badly needed a shower, my clothes were dirty, I knew I must stink. I remembered reading about the Vikings and how when somebody did something really bad, their forehead was branded with a wolf's head and they were declared an outlaw — no longer part of the human community. No one was allowed to give them food or shelter, or basically have anything to do with them. My grubby clothes, dirty face and hair were my wolf's mark.

2:32 am

I huddled in the corner of an open-sided shed in the disused railway yards, and tried to direct my attention away from my dark and defenseless position and my rumbling stomach, and on to the new lead with the Angel.

3:13 am

It was raining. I dragged over a few sheets of rusting corrugated iron and leaned them against the poles that held up the shed. They stopped some of the driving rain hitting me. I pulled my sleeping bag up tight and tried to keep dry. The roar of the trains under the wind and rain kept me awake for a long time, until finally I fell asleep, too tired to care.

5:59 am

I sat up, sore from lying on the hard ground. The recurring nightmare had shaken me from sleep once again. The white toy dog, the screaming child and the crushing weight of desolation . . . Why was this plaguing me?

My sleeping bag was soaked. My right shoulder was still aching and swollen. It just wasn't healing. I hoped it wasn't infected.

I got up, rolled the sleeping bag and left it tucked into the corner of the shed. I'd only managed a couple of hours sleep, but had to get moving.

6:23 am

The sky was lightening, and a few people were moving around the city streets already. I walked quite a distance from the railway yards and found myself in an alley where a storekeeper was unloading fruit and vegetables from the back of a pickup. He vanished inside the store, wheeling a dolly. He deftly let the roller down with his foot, leaving a box of grapes sitting outside on the sidewalk.

When I was in my first year at school, I pinched Tommy Garibaldi's airplane pencil sharpener when he wasn't looking. He was the kind of kid that always came to school with the coolest, newest things that everyone else wanted. Before I took it I figured he wouldn't even miss it, but I felt so bad about it afterwards that I snuck back into class during recess to put it back in his pencil case. I hadn't pinched anything since then. But now I had no hesitation. I scooped up the box of grapes and ran.

I stopped running when I reached a small park. Lorikeets were squabbling in the trees above me, and I sat down near a big gum tree, ripped the lid off the box and pounced on those grapes. I devoured them like a pig at a trough, and before long I lay back on the grass, filled to the bursting point.

8:00 am

I was in real trouble. Nearly doubled over with cramps in my stomach. Maybe the pickup guy'd left the grapes out on the street for a reason.

Served me right for stealing them, I guessed.

I resented the crowd of school kids in the

distance, hanging around the bus stop making jokes and talking while I rolled around alone under some tree, in some park, in some place, in absolute agony.

How would my mum feel if she knew her kid was lying in a park, sick as a . . .

Eventually the cramping eased up, and I dragged myself further under some bushes where I couldn't be seen, and slept.

11:48 am

I jumped awake. Something rustled in the bushes around me. I kept still and listened carefully before turning to look.

"Yeah, it's a man in there."

"Shhh, he's waking up."

"I'll get him with this one. Watch this!" said another voice.

A stone flew through a gap in the bushes and hit the back of my head.

"Bull's-eye! Take that, bum!"

I could hear the slapping sound of high fives. Slowly, I turned my head and saw three pairs of small, shiny black school shoes. I didn't care who saw me, I was furious. How could they think it was OK to treat me, another person, like that? I leapt to my feet, emerging upright out of the bushes like a beast.

"GRRRRRR!"

They took off instantly, screaming.

"This could be you one day!" I yelled out to them.

I stood there in shock, shaking my head, as they quickly disappeared. I thought again of the wolf's mark. So many people in the city wandered around wearing it.

11:53 am

My cell phone was ringing somewhere back in the bushes, and I scrambled to find it. "Hello?" I asked, not recognizing the phone number. Bright sunlight streamed down, and sweat from the heat of the day and my anger poured off me. I moved into the shade.

"Is that Callum Ormond?" a woman asked.

Jennifer Smith? The mystery woman?

"Yes?" I said, cautiously, looking around me. There was only one little girl with her mum, on a swing on the other side of the park.

"What happened last time we were supposed to meet? You said you were going to be there."

She sounded genuinely concerned, rather than irritated, and I started to relax a bit — I'd have to stay on guard, but this was definitely not the voice of Oriana de la Force.

"I was on my way there," I said, "when something unexpected came up."

That was true enough. I wasn't sure how much to say to her. I really didn't know who this woman was.

"Look," I added. "I thought you'd set me up. How can I know it's OK to trust you?"

I could hear her breathing on the other end of the line. I hoped she wasn't trying to find just the right lie to deliver to me.

"I don't know what I can tell you, Cal. I just know that your father had such big, warm, honest eyes, even in the midst of his devastating illness. He really wanted me to reach out to you. I put the photo he had of you in his wallet by the side of his bed — the one of the two of you by the car at the airfield, standing there with matching grins — and I held his hand and promised him I'd do whatever I could to help."

I knew exactly what photo she was talking about. It was taken at air cadets, not that long before he left for Ireland.

"So what do you want to see me about?" I asked. "Did you see Dad's drawings from his time at the hospice?"

"I did," she said, and I believed her. "But we

can talk about that when we meet."

"Did he ever say anything about something called the Ormond Singularity?"

"I don't think so. He was so sick by the time he came to the hospice. He was very difficult to understand sometimes."

"You said you had something for me?" I said, recalling our earlier discussion. "What is it?"

"I don't want to talk about it over the phone."

I could hear the fear in her voice.

"I'll explain when I meet you, Cal. I know this is a dangerous situation. I know it is not easy for you, but it's not easy for me either."

"So where are you thinking?" I asked.

"I'm working at the zoo at the moment, and I think it will probably be safe for both of us if we meet there. I can answer all your questions then."

"OK. When?"

"Sunday, the 28th?"

It would have to do. I'd have to wait.

"What time?" I asked, impatient to meet her.

"4:30? I'll be finished up by then."

"Whereabouts?"

"Do you know the sundial?"

I did. It was a famous meeting point in the zoo. "I'll be there," I said.

She hung up, and I put my phone away. This

woman had *known* Dad — had *seen* the drawings. I could feel hope returning. Maybe she'd helped Dr. Edmundson clear out Dad's stuff. What did she have for me? My pulse was racing with excitement.

With every new piece of information, my dad's secret was coming just that little bit closer . . . Despite the weak feeling, my stomach cramps had left me, along with the fury I'd felt earlier at the stone-throwing brats. In that moment, I felt like I could deal with anything.

12:26 pm

My phone rang again, and I snatched it up.

"I've just seen your pic' of that Angel! The Ormond Angel! Now we've got a real link to your family name," said Boges. "You've got to get out to the country as soon as you can and talk to that old great-uncle of yours before he takes off for the great landing strip in the sky!"

"Yeah, you're right. Although he might have flown there already."

"Not so, my man. He is still very much with us. Your mum mentioned him the last time I saw her. She'd already contacted him, hoping you'd turned up there."

"Then it's just as well I didn't."

"This Ormond Angel breakthrough is really

something. However . . ."

I knew he was thinking of saying something about not trusting Winter. I didn't want to hear it. Yeah, she'd done another disappearing act after the big reveal, but I didn't care. I wasn't going to tell him that.

"So did you already know about this Piers dude?" Boges asked.

"Dad mentioned some relative of his, ages ago — a great-great-uncle or a distant cousin or something — who'd died in World War I. This must be him. You mightn't be able to see the inscription along the bottom of the window in the photo I sent you, but it says he was killed in 1918."

Boges whistled down the line. "Your dad must have found out about the stained glass window when he was in Ireland. But by the time he came back, he was too sick to follow it up. Or explain what it means for the DMO."

"So he drew the Angel," I said, almost thinking aloud, "and enclosed the drawing with that letter he wrote to me. He *did* say he'd explain what it was about when he got home. He probably couldn't wait to get back and check the memorial out, but he never got that chance. He drew it a second time —" I said.

"Because it's really important," Boges

interrupted. "I told you that already."

I could hear the excitement in his voice. "I'll go and research this Piers Ormond guy. If he was important enough to have the stained glass window dedicated to him, he must be important enough to have earned a mention somewhere else."

"Boges," I said, changing the subject, "I'm meeting the mystery woman on the 28th. The nurse who knew Dad."

"Jennifer Smith? I know who you're talking about. How can you trust her after the last time? You were pretty sure she'd set you up. She promised to deliver and then you were grabbed."

"I know she's not Oriana de la Force, if that's what you're thinking. She talked about Dad in a way only an honest person could. And besides, I did all right last night — Winter Frey delivered the goods, and now we both know about Piers Ormond."

"I'm sorry, buddy, but I still don't like the sound of her. You be careful. How do we know she hasn't gone running straight back to Sligo?"

"She's known about that Angel since she was a little kid. And as far as we know, she hasn't told him about it. Otherwise he'd have recognized the Angel when he saw the drawing. Besides," I said, "she doesn't even like Sligo. I don't think she's interested in helping him."

"That's what she says."

I pictured Winter and her intense, dark eyes and the way she looked at me so confidently, as if she had nothing to fear from me.

But Boges was right. I couldn't know for sure.

"So when can I see that Angel?" Boges asked. "I can't wait to get a decent look at it."

"Tomorrow? Around 12:30?"

"Cool."

The little girl who'd been on the swing at the other end of the park leapt off the seat and ran to her mum in a way that reminded me of Gabbi.

"Boges, how's Gabbi?"

"Sorry, my man, there's no news, but she's still hanging on like a real fighter."

My jaw tightened — I had to be strong for Gabbi's sake. I couldn't help but think of all the times I'd made her cry when she'd annoyed me. I used to run away from her and hide, and she wouldn't know where I was, and she'd fall in a heap on the floor and wail, thinking she'd been left all alone. I wished like anything that I'd been a better brother to her.

I was determined to somehow sneak into the intensive care ward and see her.

"And Mum?" I asked.

"She came by our place again last night. I told

her that I still didn't know where you were. That was the truth – I didn't know. You could have been anywhere."

"Did she look all right?"

"She's really thin, and still kinda unfocused. She's not great, dude, but she's just about moved out of your place now. Rafe's around there most of the time, helping her pack up the house."

My reaction to hearing about Rafe was so different from just a couple of weeks ago. At least now I knew he had good intentions and would take care of Mum. I'd hoped that having the house in her name might have cheered her up.

"There's been a tough-looking guy hanging around my place," continued Boges. "Wears a red tank top. He's tried to follow me a couple of times too."

"Red tank top? With a Chinese symbol on it?"

"You know him too?"

"Boges, you're gonna have to be even more careful than ever – he's one of Sligo's gorillas. Please make sure you're never followed by him. If he gets hold of me, I'm a goner. Last time he had me he was shoving me into the oil tank."

"See? I told you that Winter Frey couldn't be trusted," said Boges.

"Huh? What's she got to do with it?"

"She's part of the Sligo attempted murder club, dude. None of them have a conscience."

"If she'd betrayed me," I said, "Red Tank Top would already know where I was and not be hanging around your place trying to get a lead."

Boges grunted. He knew I had a point.

22 FEBRUARY

313 days to go . . .

Cenotaph
Memorial Park

12:23 pm

Boges was already at the cenotaph when I arrived. He was standing there, staring up at the Angel, completely blown away.

"That is an awesome angel!" he said, without taking his eyes off it. "It's just like your dad drew."

We stood together in the cool interior of the cenotaph. The bright sun shone brilliantly through the stained glass angel, lighting the cement floor below with patches of color — yellow and blue, red and green. We squinted our eyes and read the dedication to the fallen soldier.

Boges put his sunglasses on. "There's something small beneath the gas mask. Something green and gold. Remember we thought that there was some sort of medal in your dad's drawing?"

"Yeah," I said, pulling the Angel drawing out of the folder. "You can just make out an oval shape beneath the gas mask in the drawings."

"This guy was really unlucky," said Boges, "to be killed in the last year of the Great War."

"*Unlucky* seems to be something my family does well."

"If we follow the clues your dad left for us," Boges tapped the drawings, "the luck of the Ormonds will change for the better."

"I hope so, Boges." *An astounding discovery*, my dad had said. Surely that would mean change for the better.

12:48 pm

"Thanks for keeping an eye on my family," I said, as Boges was leaving.

"Aw, it's nothing. Your mum says she likes me visiting. She says that seeing me makes things feel more normal. You know, sometimes she is almost like her old self. You kind of see that knowing sparkle in her eye, but just as quickly as it appears, it disappears."

Boges started scratching his head. "I got here today by sneaking over Mrs. Sadler's back fence instead of walking out the front door. Don't know how long it will take for them to wake up to me."

Boges gave me his lunch and his money for the school field trip that day — a repeat visit to the observatory. Boges didn't need a field trip for a reason to go there.

"Today I'd rather go to the library for free," he said, "and start digging around for information about Piers Ormond."

"Why did they call it *The Great War*?"

"There'd never been anything like it."

Boges jumped back suddenly from the rusty gates.

"What is it?"

He grabbed me and dragged me back inside. "Don't look now, but see that guy near the entrance to the park? I'm sure he's the guy from the car that's been scoping out my place."

"Who? Red Tank Top?"

"No, another guy. I wasn't sure if I was just being paranoid about this guy when I spotted him outside my house, but I think it'd be a little too much of a coincidence to run into him here in the park. He must have followed me." Boges started scratching his head again. "I thought I was careful. I'm so sorry, dude."

"Forget it. We'll figure a way around this."

I took a quick look and sure enough, there was a big guy lurking outside wearing a dark suit jacket over a T-shirt, black jeans, sneakers and sunglasses.

"If he comes over this way, he'll see you," I said, looking around the edge of the cenotaph entrance. "And he's got the place stitched up — there's no other way out of here."

A tall iron fence with seriously sharp-looking, spear-like tops surrounded the park. There was no way anyone'd be able to get over that, let alone Boges.

I thought fast. "It's *you* he's been told to follow," I said. "Chances are that even though he *thinks* he knows what I look like, I'm very different from how I look in the photos on TV and in the papers."

I pictured the clean-cut schoolboy photo on the police poster I'd seen while waiting for Winter the other night. I sure didn't look like that anymore.

"I'll go straight up to him. That would be the last thing he'd expect a fugitive to do. I'll distract him while you go around behind him. By the time he figures out that he's lost you, it'll be too late."

1:06 pm

"Got a light, Mister?" I asked, sidling up to the big man.

"Disappear, kid," he snarled, from behind his wraparound sunglasses.

"How about a dollar then, Mister?"

I was dimly aware of Boges making a wide arc around the park and heading for the entrance behind the big stooge who was scowling and trying to pretend I wasn't there.

"Come on," I said, "just one dollar. That's not much to ask from a guy like you, is it?"

"Get away from me!" He lunged at me, but I was ready for him and ducked out of his reach.

He tried to grab me again, and this time I started running. I could see Boges slipping past behind him and out of the park, quickly vanishing up the street and around the corner onto the main road.

The big stooge stopped coming after me and yelled from a distance before turning around and heading towards the cenotaph building.

He had disappointment coming his way.

But then I saw him stop, turn back and look at me. He pointed at me, pulled out his cell phone and began walking away.

Internet cafe

1:23 pm

I tried to control my puffed-out breath before I stepped into the internet cafe. I wondered what the big man in the suit jacket was doing now. He'd recognized me, I was pretty sure, and now he was probably letting Sligo know that I was in the area. I took a quick look around. The place was crowded, but I found a free desk and chair and I logged on, all the time keeping a watch out the window to the street. I'd have to move on quickly.

I knew there was a back door where the bathrooms were, so if anyone came in here after me I could be out the door and over the fence at the back in triple-quick time.

I pulled out one of Boges's sandwiches. Mrs. Michalko had used some kind of sausage stuff I'd never eaten before, and I wolfed it down without thinking too much about it. As I had a look around the desk for a piece of scrap paper to make notes on, I found something that set my heart racing yet again . . . a sticker on the hard drive next to me with my face on it! It was like a smaller version of the poster I'd seen a few days ago, only it had some internet cafe alert, and something about my blog address, and a more recent picture of me from a security camera! I instantly shut my computer down and prepared for a hasty exit.

As I stood up from my chair and glanced around me, I saw that the stickers were everywhere! On every computer! On the desks!

On the walls! In front of every single person in there!

I was out the back door and over the fence like a blur.

2:09 pm

How would I get information now? My picture was probably in every internet cafe in the city and the state! I didn't even get a chance to check my page.

📱 boges. my pic is all over internet cafe! NEW pic. must have taken it from security camera. just got out in time. didn't get any info. u?

📱 dude! that sucks. in library now. nothing 2 exciting on blog. let u know if anything changes. found the riddle the sphinx used on her victims . . . what goes on 4 legs, then 2 legs, then 3 legs?

📱 i give up.

📱 . . . a human being. first as a baby we crawl on 4 legs, then as adults we walk on 2. finally as old people we walk with a cane. 3 legs!

📱 u reckon those numbers 4, 2 & 3 are clues to dad's puzzle?

📱 could be. don't forget the number 5 in the drawing of the old cupboard or door or whatever it is. that gives us 2, 3, 4 & 5. meaning?

📱 once I caught a fish alive.

📱 cal, ur hilarious. (i'm being sarcastic, in case u can't detect my tone by sms.)

5:13 pm

I'd been slowly making my way back towards St. Johns Street, hoping that the place was empty. I'd have to wait until it was dark before actually trying to get in there. I wasn't looking forward to it, but I was so happy to be heading away from the drain and the railway yards.

I kept my head down, but occasionally I'd scan the people around me, wondering if I'd ever see that kid again — the one who looked exactly like me. Then I'd start to wonder whether I'd imagined the whole thing — seeing double, or something.

7:12 pm

I listened again on the porch. All was still and quiet. Whoever had moved in had moved out again.

I crawled up through the hole in the floor and collapsed. It was a strange feeling to feel such relief at being in this dump. Almost anything'd have been better than the drain.

I had more room, a soft glow of candlelight,

my little radio playing softly, and I'd found a can of beans I'd forgotten I'd hidden away.

📱 boges. i'm back at the mansion. b round any time soon?

📱 i'll see what i can do in the next couple of nights. hang tight.

26 FEBRUARY

309 days to go . . .

Hideout
38 St. Johns Street

12:02 pm

"Sorry, dude, but I've only got a few minutes," said Boges. "I think Mum's getting suspicious. I don't *think* she would say anything to the police, but . . . she could slip up without meaning to. I don't want my charm to fade with the teachers at school, either. My grades are still up, so they're pretty cool when I rock up to class late, or . . . not at all, but they could start seeing it as arrogance if I do it too much."

He unloaded his backpack, tossed me a black cap, a charged phone battery, and my new supplies: a bunch of bananas, a bag of rolls and more canned beans. He started laughing as he made a tower with the cans.

"What is it?" I asked, pulling the hat on.

"This diet of yours. It's primitive. Much more of this," he said, as he added the last can to his tower, "and you'll be swinging through the trees, jet-propelled by natural gas!"

It was so good to laugh.

"You heard from that Sligo chick?" Boges asked.

"Winter. No."

"Probably a good thing. Anyway I gotta go, but I'll keep you updated on your blog and let you know if I have any DMO strokes of genius — it's bound to happen, let's face it. And here," he said, handing me two twenty-dollar bills, "I fixed Mr. Addicot's laptop for him. He gave me sixty bucks!"

"Thanks a lot. If it wasn't for you, Boges, I'd have been forced into turning myself in a long time ago."

"I know you'd do the same for me," said Boges. "Forget about it."

27 FEBRUARY

308 days to go . . .

2:12 pm

I'd spent the whole morning in the library, but no one had seemed to pay any attention to me. Boges and I had both been trying to connect the numbers 2, 3, 4 and 5 to the range of clues we already had, but even his brain couldn't come up with anything. I went over all the connections we'd made in the drawings so far, but I couldn't get anything new. The Ormond Singularity remained as unfathomable as ever.

As I walked back from the library, I was starting to feel like I was just another face in the crowd. All I had to do was stay low and quiet and keep on the track of the dangerous mystery of the Ormonds. Maybe tomorrow Jennifer Smith'd give me the break I needed. It sounded easy. Somehow, I knew it wasn't going to be.

28 FEBRUARY

307 days to go . . .

Bus depot

3:20 pm

It was hot, and I was starting to get paranoid about my appearance again. I pulled my hat down low.

I was threading my way through the lines of people for the 3:30 bus to the zoo when I saw something that made me jump with fright. Red Tank Top! What was he doing here?

I immediately ducked into a doorway, peering around the edge of the corner to watch him.

He was showing a photo to people as they passed by. I was sure that it was me he was asking about, and after seeing the picture in the internet cafe, I was pretty sure he'd have something fairly up-to-date.

People walked on by, shaking their heads. They hadn't seen the psycho kid. It was clear

Sligo had him there searching for me. Worse still, he was standing right next to the door of the zoo bus. I'd have to walk past him to get on board. I could hear the announcement saying the bus was about to depart. If I missed this one, I'd miss my meeting, and maybe my last chance.

Desperate, I searched for a way around him. I had to get on that bus. Something I'd thought about the other day flashed into my mind — a technique I'd read about called "hiding in plain sight." It required a lot of boldness and a simple prop to make you practically invisible.

Now was my chance to see if it was actually true. Would it work? If it didn't, I was in big trouble. I knew what Sligo would do to me if he got hold of me again.

Keeping one eye firmly on Red Tank Top, I edged over towards a very full trash can. Beside it someone had dumped several boxes. I grabbed one of the boxes, quickly folded its lid down, put it on my shoulder as if it contained something, and with the cardboard hiding most of my face, joined the line getting on the bus, my heart thudding.

I could hear Red Tank Top's voice from behind the cover.

". . . considered very dangerous," I heard him

saying as I stepped past, so close he could have *touched* me.

". . . I've been hired by the family to find him . . ." he continued, as I stepped up to the bus, keeping the box on my shoulder. The liar!

I glimpsed him turning away from my direction with the photo, so I quickly dropped the box and edged onto the bus as the driver was busy giving change to one of the passengers. I darted unnoticed into a seat at the back.

I slunk down as the bus pulled away from the curb, and my hunter.

City Zoo

4:15 pm

I waited at the ticket window at the end of a small line of people, worried about the passing time. We'd arranged to meet at the sundial at 4:30. I still had fifteen minutes.

4:21 pm

When it was my turn at the ticket window I was shocked at how expensive the entrance fee was. I felt so stupid, but I'd guessed it was only going to be a few dollars. Like a kid, I showed the woman all the money I had — small change plus a ten-dollar bill left over from the cash Boges had given me. I didn't have enough.

"Please," I tried to explain, "I'm only going to meet someone at the sundial. I'm not going in to look at any animals. If you'd just let me in for this much?"

"You got a student card?"

"Um, no, not on me."

Sure, here's my student card, I thought. *I'm Callum Ormond. 15 years old. Armed and dangerous. Let me into your stupid zoo.*

"Look, I can't let you in unless you pay the full price. If I were to give discounts to everyone, the zoo would go broke. And then who would take care of the animals?"

"Please," I begged, "I'm not asking you to do it for everyone, just for me. Just this once," I argued, noticing the time on the wall clock behind her. If I hurried I'd make it, but there was little time for delay. "Please. It's almost the end of the day."

Her face reddened. "I don't make the rules! You should have arranged to meet somewhere else! That's the price!" She pointed to the amount on the sign above her window. "And you haven't got it. End of story."

She peered around me and gestured to the

couple behind me in the line. I gathered up my money, shoved it back in my pocket and walked towards the entrance. Security guards were there taking people's tickets, one on each side of the gate. There was no way I could sneak through.

4:28 pm

If I failed to turn up a second time, no matter what excuse I came up with, it could mean the end of my chance to speak to Jennifer Smith — the last link to my dad. I couldn't bear to lose her. There *had* to be a way in.

I walked away from the entrance area and turned down the road that ran alongside the zoo. There was no way I could climb over the tall metal fence that separated the grounds of the zoo from the road. I kept walking until I came to a turn in the road where a big tree grew hard against the fence. This was my last shot.

Hoisting myself up and trying to avoid the barbed wire running along the top of the wall was hard. I grabbed at the tree's branches with one hand and carefully placed my other hand underneath the barbed wire strands on top of the wall. I had to throw my hoodie across the barbs to give me some protection as I hauled myself over. I felt lucky that I'd done a lot of junior athletics — so many skills

I never thought I'd need were really coming in handy in this life on the run.

I threw my backpack into the bushes below, near a few rocks and a small pool. I estimated the drop to be about twelve feet, so I slowly let myself down the wall so that I didn't have quite so far to fall. I landed hard and broke my fall as best I could, remembering to keep my legs relaxed and soft. I rolled over a few times before picking myself up and grabbing my backpack.

I took a quick look around and saw nothing but more bushes and the pool. It looked like I'd landed in one of the old, abandoned enclosures.

4:43 pm

Now all I had to do was find my way out of this enclosure, make it to the sundial, meet Jennifer and find out what she had for me.

I was late, but hopefully not too late.

Apart from a small, grilled door in the wall behind me — and I didn't want to go in there in case I ran into a keeper — I couldn't see any way out unless I climbed up the rocky wall across from me and pulled myself onto the wide sidewalk of the zoo above. There were people walking back and forth along there, but I was too busy making my way through the scrub to pay much attention to them.

I had just started climbing the rocks when I heard people calling out from above. This wasn't what I wanted — to be spotted by a whole bunch of people. I ducked down. People were yelling at me, pointing and shouting, but because they were all shouting together, I couldn't make out what they were actually saying. I pulled my phone out and checked the time. I couldn't waste too much time hiding out down there in the bush. I needed to get to the sundial.

4:48 pm

I could see people pulling out their cell phones and taking pictures of me! It would only be a matter of minutes before my identity was blown. Surely they hadn't recognized me from such a distance? Didn't they have better things to do? Like looking at the animals?

Just as I was about to turn all my attention to getting out of there, without a care for who was watching, I saw something that first made my heart drop, then race. Up there on the ground above, in the middle of the shouting crowd and grinning like a hyena, was Sligo's man, Red Tank Top! He must have found someone who'd noticed me getting onto the bus earlier. I searched frantically for another way out.

It looked like I had only one option — trying my luck with that grilled feeding door in the wall I'd seen earlier.

The crowd was going crazy, as if I was some sort of wild animal myself. Maybe someone *had* recognized me, but all I could think of was Red Tank Top and how to get away from him and make my meeting. I *had* to get to that meeting! And I had to shake him somehow!

It was the tone of fear in the shouts from the crowds that made me finally pay attention to what they were trying to tell me.

Slowly, the words penetrated my mind.

"Look out!" someone was calling. "Get out of there! For heaven's sake get out of there! There's a —"

It was the last word I couldn't quite catch.

Cautiously, I stood up.

And that's when I saw him in front of me, mere feet away.

I froze and so did he, stopping dead in his tracks, raising his huge head higher to stare at me with merciless yellow eyes — a massive lion, golden brown with a black mane.

From a long way away came the sounds of the crowd that had gathered on the road above the lion's den, and then I could no longer even hear those. I forgot about Red Tank Top and the danger he represented. Every fiber, every cell in my body, was concentrating on the huge beast standing in front of me, black-tufted tail swishing to and fro. The whole world seemed to be reduced to the two of us. That's all I could see, all I could focus on.

I felt adrenaline flood me with its icy strength — flight or fight. There was no way I could fight this animal. One thump from those great paws and my bones would be crushed. Flight was the only alternative, and yet I knew that the minute I turned and ran, the massive predator would do the same. Four legs can outrun two legs any day.

Without taking my eyes from the huge beast, my heart beating hard, sweating all over, I started to back away, one foot behind the other, trying to fix the lion where he was with my gaze, moving only my feet while I carefully retreated. I knew if I tried to climb back over the wall I'd come over, he would pull me down like a kitten pulling a piece of string. My only hope was making it to the door in the wall behind me. A sound like thunder made me jump, and I was shocked at the power of his growl. His tail lashed faster, and he hunkered down, wriggling his hindquarters from side to side just like a cat about to spring at a bird.

I increased the speed of my retreat. This

seemed to activate the lion. He gave a mighty roar, and I knew he was about to jump on me.

I turned and ran to the grilled gate, trying to open it.

It wouldn't open!

From somewhere came the wailing of an alarm siren. That shocked me into realizing that I was trying to open the door the wrong way. I wrenched it open! I raced through, but just as I slammed it shut behind me, something crashed against me, hitting my leg!

The lion's roar so close to my ear was deafening. I dared to turn around and saw to my horror that the huge beast had crashed right up against the gate. I prayed that it would hold fast under his massive bulk. He dropped down and stood there, glaring at me through the steel mesh, roaring with rage.

4:59 pm

I was in a small holding pen with another door at the other end. I raced through it into a wide corridor, away from the roaring lion. The alarm was deafeningly loud down there. Any moment, the place would be swarming with security. Red Tank Top would be hot on my tracks. I had to get away! I was running down the corridor, past empty offices and laboratories, when I myself roared in pain. I looked down and was horrified to see a huge bloodstain seeping through the back of my jeans. Through the rip in the denim, I could see a deep gash, welling with blood. The lion's claw had gotten me!

Now that the shock was wearing off, my leg was becoming excruciatingly painful. I leaned against the wall for a second, feeling helpless and confused. Was it all over? I was trapped, just like the lion I'd faced a moment ago. I didn't know where to go, and there was no one I could turn to for help. The cell phone pictures of me would be identified by now and making their way into TV news reports, police bulletins and newspapers. I'd completely screwed up my second meeting. Completely screwed up. But right now, I couldn't do a thing about it. I staggered into an empty room and collapsed into a chair, trembling all over.

5:10 pm

I seemed to be in some sort of storage area. Under piles of boxes, I could see old sinks with curved faucets. Maybe this was one of the laboratories. I caught sight of a box from a pharmaceutical company and peeled at the label. Beneath a lengthy scientific name was a phrase which caught my eye — *pre-loaded tranquilizing syringes.*

That's what I need, I thought bitterly. A tranquilizer.

But the insistent sound of the alarm brought me to my senses. That wasn't the answer. I needed to stay alert and vigilant. I needed to stay at least one jump ahead of Sligo and Oriana de la Force. I needed to keep focused on escaping.

5:15 pm

I could hear voices approaching. I lurched over to the counter, picked up the box of syringes and stuffed them in a pocket of my backpack. I looked around for some painkillers, but found nothing.

I had to keep moving. And even though I felt like I couldn't move, I forced myself to keep going. I hoped Jennifer Smith would believe I wanted to see her.

I started down the corridor, ducking into another empty room when I heard voices.

The guy, a zoo official, started coming after me. I had no choice. Despite the pain in my leg, I made a sudden turn and ran back the way I'd come. Behind me, I heard him shouting and yelling into his two-way radio for reinforcements. Blood squelched in my sneakers as I raced away.

At the other end of the corridor I found a locked door. Desperately, I looked around for another way of escape, ducking into an empty office to the right of the locked door. The windows were also locked, and the air conditioning was humming. I picked up a chair, and acting on instinct, I brought it down on the locked window. Hoping to delay my pursuers a little more, I darted to the door of the office, slamming it shut and locking it from the inside. Avoiding the shattered glass, I threw my torn hoodie over the jagged edges of the window frame and hauled myself out of the window, dropping to the ground about two yards below. The jolt of the drop to the ground shot agonizing pain up through my leg.

I staggered to my feet and looked around. I had landed on a narrow path between two buildings. Here, the sound from the alarm was a little softer, but I knew that the zoo would be crawling with security and, by now, the police.

5:21 pm

The pain really hit me as I ran limping down the narrow path past the other buildings. One of the buildings nearby was a trailer, with a narrow porch at the front where a line of gumboots and work boots stood in an uneven row. Hanging above them were several wet-weather jackets and coats. I limped up the two steps. I grabbed one of the dark green keeper jackets and a pair of tall gumboots. I hoped they'd hide the blood that now soaked one leg of my jeans. I pulled my sneakers off and pulled the boots on, wincing as I pushed my injured leg into one of them.

Awkwardly, I crept to the end of the porch and peered around the corner of the building.

I could hear people talking as they headed towards the exit, fragments of conversations about what they'd seen in the lion's den.

"He couldn't have gotten very far," I overheard.

Another voice answered. "I've got him on my cell phone. Take a look. That's him there, in the gray hoodie."

I pulled the dark green jacket closer around me with relief and shoved my sneakers into my backpack.

I slipped by groups of officials in khaki shorts with walkie-talkies and clumped down the path towards the sundial – not even slowing to see if there was anyone there that could have been Jennifer Smith – past family groups with kids in strollers and a school group with their teacher. I was completely driven by fear, pain and the almost hopeless desire to escape unseen.

As quickly as I could, I hobbled down the path on legs that were shaking, blending in with the crowds who were already streaming towards the exit.

5:34 pm

I hobbled out of the entrance and onto the road within a group of senior kids from a rural school. I pretended to be part of the group, walking close to them, cowering beneath their happy chatter and teasing. No one challenged me in my dark green jacket, or saw the pain of my leg on my face, although I got some stares because of my oversized gumboots. I kept scanning around for Red Tank Top, but I couldn't see him.

My leg was throbbing, and every step killed me. Would Jennifer ever trust me again? If I'd been alone, I probably would have fallen to the floor and bawled with pain and frustration.

5:52 pm

Hidden in some bushland near the zoo, I raised my leg to stop the bleeding and tried to rest and recover a little before finally wrapping it as best I could with a ripped-up shirt.

I peered out from my hiding place and saw that police had gathered over by the zoo entrance, which was now cordoned off with tape.

At least I was on this side of the tape.

I had no choice but to suck up the pain, look as above suspicion as possible, and join the short line of people waiting for the last bus back to the city.

The rumbling of a helicopter thundered through the sky as the bus pulled away from the zoo, freeing me, for now, from capture.

Emergency Ward
Sacred Heart Hospital

7:05 pm

I quickly filled out a form – with a fake name, of course. Tom – for my dad – and Mitchell – the name of the first dog we had when I was little.

Maybe I was stupid to think that I could walk off the street and into a public hospital, but I felt far enough away from the attack at the zoo to be safe. Safe enough.

Or maybe it was because I'd lost a lot of blood and was light-headed. Too light-headed to think properly?

The bleeding had finally eased when I was called, shortly after signing in, by a doctor whose jeans I could see under the short white jacket she was wearing.

I sat up on one of the examination tables, while she cleaned out my wound, gave me a shot of painkiller and stitched the injury. I noticed how she kept looking at the wound and frowning.

She went about her work in silence until it

came time to give me another injection.

"Tell me again," she said, "about the big black dog."

"Is that for rabies?" I asked, wincing at the sting.

"No," she said. "There's no rabies in Australia at the moment, but animal bites can turn septic. Anyway, don't worry about that, just tell me more about that dog."

I repeated my story of the big black dog. Except this time I made the story a bit more interesting, adding in a soccer ball I was kicking.

"You were kicking a soccer ball in those gumboots?"

"Stupid, eh?" I replied. *So stupid . . . Surely I could have come up with a more believable story.*

She secured the bandages with a clip and straightened up. "You'll need to keep this dry. No baths or showers for the next three days."

I assured her that wouldn't be a problem.

"These bandages will need changing in a day or two. I'll give you a letter for your doctor."

I nodded as she wrote up the doctor's letter. Through the open doorway I saw a doctor on a phone, looking around quite tensely. He gestured to someone, and before I knew it, hospital security had approached him. The police must have contacted them about me. I had to get out.

I stood up to leave as the doctor called me back.

"Tom," she said, and I almost didn't respond to the unfamiliar name. "I worked in Kenya for *Médecins sans Frontières*. I've seen those injuries before. That's not a dog's bite. Only the claws of a big cat can make marks like that."

"It wasn't a cat, it was a dog."

"I'm not talking *domestic* cat."

There was a silence while we stared at each other.

"Gotta go. Thanks," I said, hurrying out, right past the doctor that had been talking to security.

9:09 pm

I wandered around aimlessly in the dark, far from the hospital, my body aching with loneliness. It was more painful than my stitched-up leg. I thought again of the lion and his massive eyes, the way they stared coldly into mine . . . before he reached out and tore my leg open.

I saw something in those eyes that made me uneasy. I couldn't help but wonder if I would eventually crack and live up to the "psycho kid" tag I'd been given. I was afraid that being trapped and isolated could do it. Maybe sooner rather than later.

I noticed a pay phone across the street and was instantly drawn to it. I hobbled over to it and dialed Rafe's number. I couldn't use my cell phone for fear of being traced.

"Hello?" Rafe's voice came down the crackly line.

I thought of him on the other end, with my dad's face.

"Who is this?" he asked. "Is that you, Cal?" His voice quickly warmed. "Look, son, please come home. Your mother needs you. We all need you." He paused for a moment, waiting for me to say something, but I just couldn't.

"Are you still there?" he asked again. "Say something, please?"

"Hi," I finally whispered. It was all I could muster.

"Cal! You're OK! Please come home."

"Cal?" he said again, after a long silence.

"Who is it?" I heard Mum in the background.

But I'd hung up before anyone had a chance to say anything more.

9:38 pm

There was no way I'd hear from Jennifer again, I convinced myself. I'd been hoping she'd call me, ever since I left the zoo. Give me a chance to explain myself. Arrange to meet somewhere else, tonight. But who was I kidding? If she was going to call she would have done it by now. I'd have to go back to St. Johns and rest up.

My phone rang just as I'd given up on Jennifer Smith. I hoped it would be her. Or Boges.

"Cal, it's me. I have to see you."

It was Winter. I imagined her with her dark, floaty hair and wondered where she was calling from.

"Hi," I said, my image of her dark, floaty hair quickly transforming into the image of her creeping around Sligo's car lot, stealing car parts. Was she fooling me, like she was fooling Sligo? Somehow, even in my uncertainty, my miserable mood lessened at the sound of her voice.

"I was thinking we could meet up at the Hibiscus Cafe. It's open pretty late. We could have a quick chat and a smoothie or something?"

"You know my situation," I said, not wanting to say too much on the phone, "money-wise."

"Listen," she said, "You supply the company. I'll supply the cash. OK?" Then she giggled. "That's not quite true. Sligo will supply the cash — although he doesn't know it."

I smiled on hearing her giggle, but stopped myself.

"I saw you," I blurted out, "when you were in Sligo's car lot. You were crawling around looking into the cars and under the tarps."

"What are you talking about?"

"The car lot. The other day. I came to look for you, and I saw you there sneaking around."

"You're wrong, Cal," she said. "Why would *I* have to sneak around Sligo's?"

Forget the cute giggle, I told myself. Remember Sligo. This girl hangs around with Sligo. This girl tells lies.

"Anyway," she continued, back to her earlier, friendly tone. "There's something I need to talk to you about. Something really important. Something very dangerous."

"What is it?"

"I'll tell you when I see you. Where are you now?"

"I'm not that far from the Hibiscus Cafe. I'm just outside the —" I stopped. What was I doing? Telling Winter Frey where I was? For all I knew, Red Tank Top might have been standing right beside her, taking down notes.

"Never mind," I said, thinking fast. I *did* want to see her. But I'd have to arrange some place to meet where I could set myself up earlier — somewhere I could check out her arrival, and see whether she'd come alone. Or not.

I thought of the clock tower near Liberty Square as the perfect spot for me to watch her. It had a great view of the east side of the mall where there was another cafe that I knew would be open.

"What about meeting at the Blue Note at ten?" I asked. "Hello?" I said, puzzled, when she didn't respond. The connection must have dropped out. She was gone. I looked for her number to call back when the screeching of tires made me jump.

A black Subaru had screamed to a halt, mounting the sidewalk only feet behind me! Red Tank Top was already halfway out of the driver's seat!

And was there another person in the back seat? Someone with dark, floaty hair who'd just set me up?!

I turned and ran. I had to ignore the pain in my leg, and I hared across the road, ducking stray cars, zigzagging to the other side, ignoring the blasts of horns and the shouts of shocked and angry drivers. From the corner of my eye I could see Red Tank Top coming after me. He was fast. He was ducking and weaving the same trail as I had.

I put my head down and raced like anything down the sidewalk, knocking people out of my way, crashing around corners.

And he kept right up behind me.

I was almost at the train station. I raced to get there, hoping that I could lose him among the late-night commuters and party-goers going up and down the ramp to the dozens of platforms.

But a quick sideways twist of my head showed me that I was far from losing him. Red Tank Top was gaining on me. He was closing the gap, and he knew it. Now I could even see his evil grin as he strained to catch me. I'm right here behind you, he seemed to be saying. You're dead!

I forced my injured leg to keep working, racing along at a singeing pace. I knew only too well what would become of me if I were caught. Torture. Death. I had to outrun him.

Underground train line
Liberty Square

10:02 pm

I jumped and scrambled over the ticket barriers. I turned around to see if I was still being followed. I could see a railway attendant talking into his two-way and had no doubt he was reporting me. I kept running, my breathing coming hard, and the ache in my bad leg weakening me even further.

But I couldn't stop now.

I ran down onto the first-level platform hoping to jump on a train and free myself from my pursuer, but the train was already pulling out too fast.

More stairs led to lower platforms. I had no choice but to keep descending.

Red Tank Top thundered behind me. In a panic, I made a bad move and jumped from about halfway down the stairs. I felt the stitches burst as soon as I landed.

I howled and stumbled with pain, my wound splitting open again, but somehow I kept going.

My backpack bumped hard and heavy on my shoulders as I hit more stairs. I wanted to throw it off, but I couldn't. Everything important to me was in there.

Including a box of tranquilizing syringes!

Still racing towards the trains going to who knows where, I kept going, reaching my hand back, feeling around for the pocket in the side of my backpack where I'd hurriedly stashed the syringes back at the zoo. My fingers closed around one of them and I pulled it out, checking it as I ran. The loaded syringe, with its cone-shaped lid over the sharp end, was enclosed in a sterile plastic sleeve. I tore it open with my teeth as I ran.

Tiring now, the blood starting to rush free from my leg, I was slowing down.

I saw him come flying down the flight of stairs to the platform I was running along. Now he was at the bottom of the steps and still coming after me. Only a handful of people stood around waiting, not particularly disturbed by a kid running for his life past them. A couple of women clutched their bags closer.

A dark tunnel yawned ahead of me.

I headed into it.

My breath was coming in shorter, harder gulps. I was almost at the end of my strength.

I turned to see where Tank Top was.

I gasped in fright — he was almost on top of me! I could hear his panting, see the fury on his face, the rage in his narrowed eyes. He was going to make me pay for this chase. He could almost reach me. And my plan required that he did. I wasn't even sure that it would work, or how long before the tranquilizer would take effect.

I headed deeper into the gaping darkness of the tunnel, running along a siding that tapered ahead, narrowing until the platform finished at the tracks.

I had no choice — I jumped down and headed off into the tunnel, running as hard as I could along the tracks, where dim blue lights along the wall lit my way, and past the dark recesses of the human-sized safety alcoves placed at intervals along the tunnel.

I heard him jump down behind me with a grunt. And at that sound, I pulled off the lid of the syringe, and pretended to stumble on the tracks.

He roared with triumph and reared up, preparing to pounce on top of me.

I rolled over and held the syringe firmly pointed straight up, but hidden out of sight.

He fell on me, grabbing me with his powerful hands, and I lunged upwards with the needle, jabbing him in the neck. I depressed the plunger before he had time to even realize what was happening.

He shrieked in pain and shock. Then loomed above me again, both his hands clenched, making a powerful, martial arts-style weapon of his fists. He brought them down towards me, and I barely had the strength to move out of his way.

His fists hit the edge of the left-hand rail first, and then his body followed, rolling over the track, the needle sticking out of his neck. I saw his eyes on me and the puzzled expression in them as he tried to get up, and fell back. He blinked, opening and closing his mouth, as if to speak. But no sound came out.

Then he crashed completely, his body flopped out like a rag doll, his eyes rolled up into his head, and then he was perfectly still.

"Sleep tight," I whispered.

10:25 pm

I fell under a dim blue glow on the tunnel wall, my chest heaving. Every muscle ached and throbbed, and I could feel blood dripping from the gash in the back of my leg. Some people back on the platform had started yelling, and I knew it wouldn't be long before security turned up. They'd find Red Tank Top lying on the tracks inside the tunnel. They mustn't find me anywhere near him.

I began picking my way along the tracks, scrambling over junction boxes and safety boxes, running alongside the ties, when the rumblings of a train in another tunnel seemed to get louder.

At first I felt a cool breeze, and then there was a distinct rush of air coming towards me. The sound I could hear wasn't coming from a nearby tunnel — it was on *this* line. And it was speeding its way towards me!

Before running for the closest safety alcove, I stopped to look behind me at the lifeless shape of Red Tank Top lying unconscious on the tracks.

I hesitated, almost ignoring the urge to go back and move him, but I couldn't . . . I just couldn't leave him in the path of an oncoming train.

The sound was almost unbearable as I hobbled back to Red Tank Top's side. With all of my strength, I pushed my hands underneath him, but as I began to heave his bulky body off the tracks the blue lights suddenly disappeared. Blackness fell heavily on my eyes, and I panicked in the sudden darkness, and stumbled. Pain soared up my bad leg. The blue lights flickered, and I saw that Red Tank Top's body had rolled and tumbled off the tracks, but my blood-soaked foot had slipped between a tie and a safety box onto a metallic mesh ground . . . and become firmly wedged.

My foot was completely stuck.

The roar of the train was getting louder. I could now see its blazing lights in the distance behind me. Sweat rushed down my face as I desperately tried to free myself.

The sudden whoomp of pressured air hit my back as the train approached. Even more desperately, I tried to free myself, twisting this way then that, trying to wrench my foot out, trying to crawl off the tracks.

The train was bearing down on me. I could

even see the cabin now, above the light. The driver had spotted me!

He'd applied the brakes, and the train was screaming as he attempted to stop it.

Would I lose my leg? Or my life?

I screamed, but my voice was swallowed up by the terrible sound of the train's approaching wheels sparking against the brakes. Blazing lights blinded me. I was deafened by the screeching and the blaring horns echoing throughout the tunnel as the train thundered towards me. Frenzied, I struggled to free my trapped ankle! Straining every muscle of my body, I screamed for help!

It would never stop in time and I'd be creamed, minced on the tracks! I gave a last desperate heave, trying to escape. But my foot, trapped in the boot I'd taken from the zoo, wouldn't budge.

In slow motion, I watched the train come closer, my body frozen in horror. Time seemed to stop.

IS RACE AGAINST TIME 06:48 07:12 05:21 RACE AGAI
CE AGAINST TIME SEEK THE TRUTH... CONSPIRACY 3
E SOMETHING IS SERIOUSLY MESSED UP HERE 08:30
06 06:07 JUNE WHO CAN CAL TRUST? SEEK THE TRU
NE 06:04 10:08 RACE AGAINST TIME 02:27 08:06 10:3
E TRUTH 01:00 07:57 SOMETHING IS SERIOUSLY MES
01 09:53 CONSPIRACY 365 12:00 RACE AGAINST TIM
NE WHO CAN CAL TRUST? 01:09 LET THE COUNTDOW
NE HIDING SOMETHING? 03:32 01:47 05:03 JUNE LET
UNTDOWN BEGIN 09:06 10:33 11:45 RACE AGAINST TIM
12 05:21 RACE AGAINST TIME RACE AGAINST TIME SE
UTH... CONSPIRACY 365 TRUST NO ONE 06:07 SOME
RIOUSLY MESSED UP HERE 08:30 12:01 05:07 06:06
O CAN CAL TRUST? SEEK THE TRUTH 12:05 JUNE 06:
CE AGAINST TIME 02:27 08:06 10:32 SEEK THE TRUT
7 SOMETHING IS SERIOUSLY MESSED UP HERE 05:0
NSPIRACY 365 12:00 RACE AGAINST TIME 04:31 10:17
N CAL TRUST? 01:09 LET THE COUNTDOWN BEGIN JU
METHING? 03:32 01:47 05:03 JUNE LET THE COUNTD
06 10:33 11:45 RACE AGAINST TIME 06:48 07:12 05:2
AINST TIME RACE AGAINST TIME SEEK THE TRUTH...
S TRUST NO ONE SOMETHING IS 06:07 SERIOUSLY M
RE 08:30 12:01 05:07 06:06 06:07 JUNE WHO CAN CA
EK THE TRUTH 12:05 JUNE 06:04 10:08 RACE AGAINST
06 10:32 SEEK THE TRUTH 01:00 07:57 SOMETHING
SSED UP HERE 05:01 09:53 CONSPIRACY 365 12:00 R
IE 04:31 10:17 JUNE WHO CAN CAL TRUST? 01:09 LET
UNTDOWN BEGIN JUNE HIDING SOMETHING? 03:32 01
NE LET THE COUNTDOWN BEGIN 09:06 10:33 11:45 RA
IE 06:48 07:12 05:21 RACE AGAINST TIME RACE AGAI
EK THE TRUTH... CONSPIRACY 365 TRUST NO ONE S
07 SERIOUSLY MESSED UP HERE 08:30 12:01 05:07
IE WHO CAN CAL TRUST? SEEK THE TRUTH 12:05 JU
08 RACE AGAINST TIME 02:27 08:06 10:32 SEEK THE
57 SOMETHING IS SERIOUSLY MESSED UP HERE 05: